My Life in Smiley: I GOT THIS!
(almost . . .)

Acknowledgments

Many thanks to Clémentine Sanchez for her invaluable help, Alexandra Bentz for her trust, Samantha Thiery for her support and management, as well as the entire Smiley team.

 For Elisa and Hortense.

my Life in SMILEY®

ILLUSTRATED BY TIM JONES FOR SMILEYWORLD

I GOT THIS!

(almost . . .)

ANNE KALICKY

Andrews McMeel
PUBLISHING®

It is officially forbidden to read this masterpiece before **Saturday, April 19, 2127!**

Whoever you are, whatever your name is, if—by the greatest of misfortunes—you've stumbled upon this notebook, immediately chuck it as far away as you possibly can or . . . put it back where it belongs. If you refuse to obey this command, my punishment will be TERRIBLE: your head will become covered with pigeon turds, your eyebrows will become three times thicker, snakes will burst from your mouth, your toes will morph into spinach, and you'll feel like you have to throw up for the rest of your life!

This is your last chance to avoid becoming a horrifying monster! Never, under any circumstances, turn this page. Dispose of this journal (in a manner so that its proper owner can find it) or prepare yourself for the darkest hours of your miserable life!

(Um . . . sorry, Mom, if you find this while cleaning my room. . . . love you!)

SEPTEMBER

VACATION REPORT:

COMMENCE
BRIEFING

Dear future  human,

Here I am again . . .

after two months of well-deserved vacation. Believe me—being a teen and (future) hero isn't very relaxing. 😣

Remember last year: the mysterious graffiti on the wall of the secret passage, Raoul Kador's dirty tricks, the retirement ☠ home, the prank calls, Ramoupoulos's PE class, and the anxiety over Conrad's visit—you know, my English exchange student with the mullet? This little intro to middle school really stressed me out. By the end of June, I was totally exhausted . . . and I still haven't quite recovered. I think we should alternate between one year of school and one year of vacation, don't you? 😊

Like every time I go on vacation, I left my brilliant personal journal at home. But did you see? This time I added an even more "discouraging" warning than last year, and apparently no one touched it.

Still, I did take some discreet notes so I could catch you up on the most memorable events of my summer break . . . and I have a lot to tell you.

For starters, after the end-of-the-year party, that old slug Tom and I hung out for a bit. He tried to teach me some graffiti tricks, but I have to admit I'm a lot better at writing.

On the wall of the secret passage, Tom wrote: "M + T = blood brothers." He really wanted us to leave our mark before we went on vacation.

In July, the streets started to empty out. You could feel the mass exodus from the big cities toward the ocean beaches. Tom and I weren't so lucky. He took the train to the Basque country, in the south of France, and I headed west toward Brittany. The day before we left, we made sure our time capsule was still safe in its hiding place, buried in the vacant lot.

Then Tom gave me a present for my birthday ahead of time. I was born on August fifth. You couldn't pick a worse date— in the middle of summer vacation, when no one's around to celebrate your b-day! But the worst part is that my birthday is right after Marion's. The very next day! As in, hers is the day before! As in, just before mine! Get the picture? In case you forgot, Marion is my older sister, and she is still so annoyyyyyying!

So my sister's birthday is the fourth and mine is the fifth. I have no idea how my parents could have done such a thing to me, but the result: total disaster. I'm always second . . . I'm sure I've been cursed!

Anyway, I shouted with joy when I unwrapped Zombieland Anthology: 1 and 2. It's a guidebook to the video game that gives you all the tricks to beat the levels, survive every world, and save Earth!

THE BEST
PRESENT OF MY
ENTIRE LIFE!

That slug
is great!

I took the train to Brittany with my sisters, Marion and Lisa. Ever since Lisa ruined my plan with Naïs, I've been mad at her. 😠 WHAT A PEST! Honestly! At the end-of-the-year party I'd organized, I was within an inch of kissing Naïs when suddenly my sister blasted her favorite singer, Ben Didji. And of course when I complained the next day that this wasn't exactly the deal I'd made with Marion (who'd sworn to handle all the music HERSELF), my parents defended their little "darling Lili." Since then I've been calling Lisa "Little Diaper" because she's totally my parents' baby. 😊

On the train we ended up next to an old grandma who kept grumbling any time we moved a muscle. And it was pretty annoying, since our trip was over two hours long. I didn't even dare eat the salami sandwich wrapped in aluminum foil that my mom had packed for me. I wound up just going to sleep.

But I woke up to a message over the loud speaker:

"Maxime Cropin, please come to the restaurant car and pick up your Little Diaper."

Even if I was "relatively" incognito on this train, I had no clue what to do with myself. I looked around for Lisa: she'd disappeared. I was furious!

I wanted to race to the restaurant car, but in my rush I accidentally caught the purse of the old lady, who also woke up and began screaming <u>STOP, THIEF!</u> Total panic broke out in the train car, the ticket inspector showed up, and . . . dear future human, I'll spare you the details of this terrible misunderstanding to which I fell victim. When I finally found Lisa one hour later, she was with Marion in the restaurant car, laughing to death at her practical joke. And when I went back to my seat, the lady was sinking her dentures into <u>MY</u> sandwich!

So when we finally got to our grandparent's house, I was at my wits' end and completely starving. Luckily, Grandma Ragny had prepared her famous "pasta diphore": her super special version of spaghetti and meatballs. . . . Ta die for!

Overall, staying with Grandpa Joff and Grandma Ragny was pretty cool. For starters, my parents made an exception to the only-one-hour-of-video-games-a-day rule. 😁 Thanks to the book Tom gave me, I beat *Zombieland 2*. And guess what? At the end of the book, there was a flyer advertising a new game that looks flippin' sweet: *Dogs of Hell.* Apparently, it's about a hero who has to save his son from Lucifer's imprisonment. He has to fight the hounds that guard the gates to each level of the underworld.

Ooooh! A totally spooky game—just how I like it . . . 😛

On top of that, Grandma Ragny announced that we'd have dinner in front of the TV every night. There's nothing better than salt and vinegar chips and hot dogs while watching an old Western! 😊 Grandpa Joff and Grandma Ragny love the old classics. Grandpa has a whole collection of VHS tapes. Dear future human, you're undoubtedly wondering:

> What in the world is a VHS tape?

Well, try to imagine a kind of box that can save movies shown on TV using a machine called a "videocassette recorder." It was cutting-edge stuff back when Grandpa Joff was younger! But even in my era it's outdated, and I bet Grandpa has to be one of the last people on earth still using this funky machine.

😵

Besides that, we visited the beach, went fishing, hiked, and learned a card game from Marion called "Scum." Each player has cards and has to put down a card greater than those of the other players. The winner—whoever gets rid of all their cards first—becomes President, and the person in last place becomes . . . Scum.

If this game sounds fun to you, future human, you can probably find the rules of the game in the historical archives of the last century. At first, I wasn't really feeling it: cards aren't normally my thing, and playing with Lisa when I was still mad at her was out of the question. But in the end, the game turned out to be a darn good way to pass the time while Grandma and Grandpa were napping. I have to say, I demonstrated great strategy and skill from the very first game.

11

But one day Grandma woke up early, and when she saw us playing cards, she seemed really interested. Obviously, we didn't tell her the real name of the game. Instead, we told her we were playing "President." 😁 And since it was her first time playing, I mopped the floor with her from the get-go. I was so excited that I slipped up. 🙁

Grandma Ragny WAS NOT pleased and sent me to my room to "contemplate" how to "respect your elders." I wanted to argue and remind her about the time last year, at the retirement home, when I proved my loyalty to senior citizens. But after some thought, I decided silence was my best defense. To be honest, I'm pretty sure Grandma is just a sore loser.

While we were there, there was also a meteor shower, and that, dear future human, is something I never miss. It's the PERFECT OPPORTUNITY to wish on a shooting star, and IT WORKS!

Not that I'm superstitious or easily tricked . . . I just have past experience. One day, when I was (a lot) younger, Grandpa and Grandma insisted we visit Aunt Géromine, Grandpa Joff's sister. I didn't have anything against Aunt Géromine, but I remembered she had beehives on her patio. I was terrified I'd be stung and end up in the emergency room.

By chance, the night before, I saw a shooting star and made a wish that we wouldn't go to her house. The crazy thing is when we got to her house, there was a note on the door.

On vacation under the palm trees. Come back next year.

She'd left to go island hopping with a guy she'd fallen madly in love with only a few days before! Double shocker! 😮 But I was relieved to avoid the whole ordeal. That was when I realized there was a way to get whatever you wanted at least ONE TIME a year. 😉

After that, I did a fair amount of research online on wish making, and, with all modesty, I can say I became an expert. 😁 I learned all of the rules to guarantee that a wish will come true. I am already thinking about my next bestseller: *When You Wish upon a Star!* Anyway, since the incident with Aunt Géromine, I've stuck to the tradition. Every summer, in the beginning of August, Grandma Ragny makes a snack and we set up lawn chairs in the garden. But this year, things got a lot more complicated than expected. 😞

Dear future human, you obviously know better than anyone that stargazing demands EXTREME CONCENTRATION. But the whole family was ganging up on me. Every time I spotted a shooting star, someone else had already seen it.

So my wish had NO chance of succeeding, since there can be only ONE wish per shooting star. To make things worse, Lisa was yelling out her wishes at the top of her lungs, which totally broke my concentration. I was afraid I'd get all mixed up and make some crazy wish like, "Please make Ben Didji fall in love with me." And all four of them wouldn't stop asking me questions, so many that I had a hard time mentally reciting the formula I'd memorized ahead of time.

If I run the numbers, I bet that out of the fifteen shooting stars I saw, I made only about three valid wishes.

Get
Dogs of Hell

Kiss Naïs

Grow a beard
(and become a professional
soccer player)

OK, OK, on that star
I tried to squeeze in
two wishes.

My parents joined us right after
to celebrate MY birthday and . . . Marion's
too. I'd spent a good chunk of my summer
break trying to put the ad for *Dogs of Hell* in
plain sight where Grandma and Grandpa would
notice it. But when I blew out my twelve
candles and unwrapped my presents, I saw that
all of my efforts had failed miserably.

Grandpa and Grandma gave me a Pietro bag for school, but it wasn't exactly what I was hoping for. . . .

PIETRO SAYS, HOORAY FOR SCHOOL!

Since I'm starting German 😉 this year, I also got a bilingual dictionary from none other than Aunt Géromine. Inside I found a bookmark—or more like a piece of cardboard with bees drawn all over it. On every bee was written a name: Mireille, Giselle, Noëlle, Marcelle. . . . It scared the crap out of me! Then my parents brought out an enormous package. All of a sudden, I thought: "Sick! A new bike? A folding scooter? A motor scooter? A new video game console? The Niphon 12?"

I was just starting to make a comprehensive list of dream gifts in my head when my mom explained that the whole family had put together a giant party bag with twelve gifts for my twelfth birthday.

Inside there was:

A MINI-GOLF SET
A LIGHT-UP OWL
A CUSTOMIZED HOURGLASS
BASKETBALL SOCKS
A WOODEN PUZZLE
A MUG WITH MY BABY PICTURE ON IT
A PLUSH TOY
AN EXTENDABLE BACK SCRATCHER
GLOW-IN-THE-DARK TOILET PAPER
A HOT DOG-SHAPED NOTEPAD
A MOO BOX TOY
A FROG HEAD SLEEPING MASK

And what about Marion? Well, she got . . . a pair of LEATHER PANTS!

QUESTION time: when will I FINALLY be able to get _ADULT_ presents?

This whole birthday thing must've completely traumatized me, because the following night I had a nightmare about going back to middle school!

Naïs, will you marry me?

HA! HA! HA!

Naïs laughing

Me as a bee

Luckily, there was at least ONE thing that could salvage my unsuccessful shooting star night: the friendship and love bracelets from Lisa! My sister spent her entire vacation making all kinds of them.

She explained that you had to make a wish when you put the bracelet on your wrist, and on the day it breaks, your wish will come true. It was the perfect way to double my chances of kissing Naïs this year.
<u>I absolutely had to have one!</u>

I understood right away that she was employing the same methods of extortion that I'd used on her.

No, they're for sale!

Since she was born, I've always been a role model for Lisa . . . but it's still annoying when the student surpasses the master.

I tried to trade her my hot dog notepad and the light-up owl for a bracelet, but she said my presents were total garbage. Between us, she's got some nerve—she helped pick them out for me!

But in the end she offered me a deal: if I agreed to play "Shrimp Splash" with her at the beach, she'd give me a bracelet. This "game" consisted of jumping in the waves and yelling, "Shrimp splash!"

The first person to fall has to imitate a whale and spit water in the air. I <u>DIDN'T</u> have a choice. . . . I agreed, and she promised to give me a bracelet after I played with her at least once.

I fulfilled my promise the next day, but at one point—I don't know how—I wound up with my head in the sand. Lisa yelled, "Shrimp splash!" and I started imitating a beached humpback. And then! Guess who I saw walking along the beach with her parents? You'll never believe me: NAÏS! I'm positive it was her!

But by the time I got up and finished wiping away the salt water that was stinging my eyes, she'd disappeared.

What a coincidence, huh? There was roughly a 1-in-3.51 billion chance that we would meet, and destiny brought us within two feet of each other.

Thankfully she didn't see me, or at least I don't think she did. Dear future human, you better believe that after that, I spent A LOT MORE time at the beach hoping to see her. And I decided I needed to stack all the odds in my favor if I wanted to become a mega hunk.

In one of Marion's magazines I ran across an article that seemed promising:

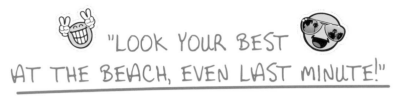

"LOOK YOUR BEST
AT THE BEACH, EVEN LAST MINUTE!"

Just what I needed! The article gave all sorts of advice to get "a firm body ASAP," "silky soft skin," "the hair of a siren," etc. I did push-ups every morning and slathered my hair and body in oil.

The result? I got sunburned all over, I never saw Naïs again, and my guns stayed the same: nonexistent. The only good news was that Lisa made me a friendship bracelet.

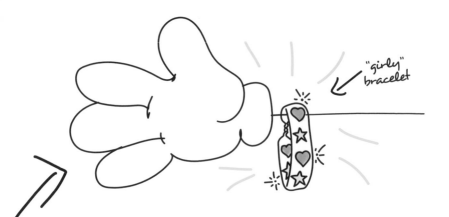

"girly" bracelet

I made my wish when she put it on my wrist. Now, "All we have to do is wait," like Grandpa Joff says when he casts his fishing line! 😊

And finally, what I've told you about so far is nothing compared to what I suspect Marion was up to. Would you believe it, future human, if I told you I'm 98.96% SURE that, during the summer, she went out with Tristan Le Bouzec—the neighbor's son? ●

The Le Bouzecs run the souvenir shop in the village, the one where I bought the key rings for my parents and Marion during fall break last year, remember?

Tristan is seventeen years old, and he's going to be a senior. He lives there in Brittany. We've known him forever because he knows how to make forts better than anyone. And, well, this summer he and Marion were stuck together like glue. I have proof!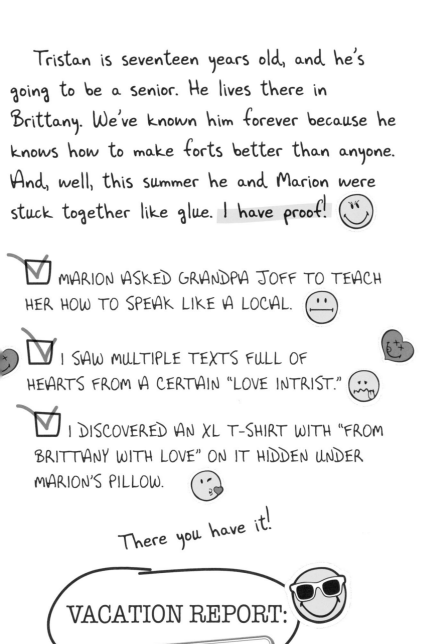

☑ MARION ASKED GRANDPA JOFF TO TEACH HER HOW TO SPEAK LIKE A LOCAL.

☑ I SAW MULTIPLE TEXTS FULL OF HEARTS FROM A CERTAIN "LOVE INTRIST."

☑ I DISCOVERED AN XL T-SHIRT WITH "FROM BRITTANY WITH LOVE" ON IT HIDDEN UNDER MARION'S PILLOW.

There you have it!

VACATION REPORT:

TERMINATE BRIEFING

Monday

At long last, in three days I start seventh grade. I have a feeling this year is going to be AWESOME! I'm sure my genius will finally be recognized. Well when I got home, there was something that dampened my mood. You see, there were two postcards waiting for me on my desk. From afar, I thought it was Tom and Naïs who had written me, and my heart starting pounding. Have I mentioned I really like Naïs? She sure is pretty. I thought about her all summer, about the kiss we almost shared and our (brief) meeting in Brittany.

But UGH! NOT AT ALL!

The first card was from Conrad, my English pen pal, and frankly he hadn't made much progress in French since he stayed at my house last April. . . .

Hapy Day of
Berth, Max!
See you soon
at me house,
on England!

MAX,
FRACE

Guess who the other card was from?
Bingo. Raoul, my ex-sworn enemy. That show-
off hadn't gotten any better either. He went
to Texas for vacation, and of course . . . he
had to rub it in.

By the way, it wasn't even a real postcard—just a cheap photograph. Tom got the same card. We figured out that this big loser sent the same photo to the whole class . . . just to look cool!

I'm crossing my fingers that Naïs didn't get his postcard. Imagine if she fell for his charms . . . for his trap, at least.

Anyway, tonight Tom and I are going to see the class lists posted at the school entrance. With a bit of luck, Raoul will be in a different class and, soon, nothing but a bad memory.

Dear future human, Tuesday

The world is cruel and unjust. . . . Life isn't worth living anymore! For the first time ever, I'm not in the same class as Tom! I don't think I'll survive. Here's what happened. Yesterday, Tom and I met at the entrance of our secret passage to go to school together.

But, as soon as we got there, we realized everyone had had the same idea. It was a battle royale to get up to the front and see the lists. As I was looking for our names, I realized the worst.

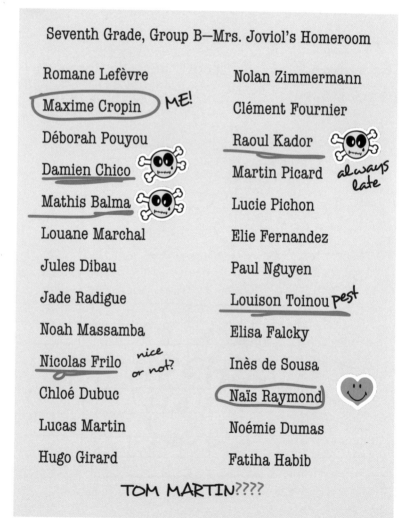

Seventh Grade, Group B—Mrs. Joviol's Homeroom

Romane Lefèvre

Maxime Cropin　ME!

Déborah Pouyou

Damien Chico

Mathis Balma

Louane Marchal

Jules Dibau

Jade Radigue

Noah Massamba

Nicolas Frilo　nice or not?

Chloé Dubuc

Lucas Martin

Hugo Girard

Nolan Zimmermann

Clément Fournier

Raoul Kador

Martin Picard　always late

Lucie Pichon

Elie Fernandez

Paul Nguyen

Louison Toinou　pest

Elisa Falcky

Inès de Sousa

Naïs Raymond

Noémie Dumas

Fatiha Habib

TOM MARTIN????

Tom was in ANOTHER CLASS! 😲 Can you believe it? What did I do to deserve this? I swear I'm cursed . . . 🙁 Instead (once again) I have to endure Raoul and two of his dimwits, Damien Chico and Mathis Balma! ☠️

I've been in bed since yesterday, unable to get up. I'm barely able to write to you. I'm a shadow of my former self. . . . Can you imagine?

I feel like an astronaut lost in deep space. All of the good my vacation did for me melted away with the terrible news. I didn't even have the guts to read the fifteen texts from Tom. This is all because of that night with the falling stars, I know it! ⭐⭐ With all of Grandpa and Grandma's distractions, I'd completely forgotten to make a wish to be in the same class as Tom. Now, for the first time since kindergarten, we'll be torn apart! 😣

A few days ago, I read an article about a billionaire who's working on a completely crazy project: <u>sending one hundred humans to Mars within ten years.</u> The guy explained that the first "colonists" would not come back to Earth and they needed to be "ready to die."

At the time I found the idea scary, but now I am totally READY to be a part of this voyage. Even right now, if I had to!

SURVIVAL KIT TO BRING TO MARS

- Salt and vinegar chips
- Pietro soap
- Sunglasses
- A picture of my parents
- Video game console + batteries
- AC unit
- My journal
- A rechargeable light
- Tom?
- My favorite comic book: Extreme Excavator

After spending twenty-four hours straight in my room, my mom finally came to see what was wrong. I spit it out. She seemed to understand my problem right away. Well . . . at least that's what I thought. But then she wanted me to do a relaxation exercise. My mom read loads of books this summer about "the art of Zen," "nonviolent communication," "full consciousness," and all of that popular hoo-ha. ⟶

CHILDREN SOFT AS PANDAS

She told me to lie down (I already was), close my eyes, and trace the outline of a castle in my mind in order to call upon all the energy inside of myself. . . . And, believe me, no matter how hard I tried, I couldn't find a single ounce of energy left within me.

Dear future human, the adults of my time are really mysterious: some do everything they can to bug you, and others want you to remain calm at all costs. Sometimes I don't understand them at all.

Finally, even with an empty stomach, I fell asleep. I have to say, Mom's cheesy cauliflower wasn't exactly calling me. . . .

The first day back in school, the first day of seventh grade. Tom and I were totally bummed. 😟

He was as upset as me about the whole thing, but the difference for Tom was that he had only ONE of Raoul's 😈 losers in his class—and he's with Célia, Naïs's friend. 😍 He did, however, remind me of one thing that boosted my spirits: 💀

NAÏS AND I ARE IN THE SAME CLASS!

That's what he was trying to text me all day long yesterday! I was so preoccupied that this wimp wasn't in my class that I didn't pay attention to the most important information!

Yesssss! Raoul, His Royal Pain in the You-Know-What, has finally returned! Yessss!

In the hallway, I spotted Raoul. He was hard to miss. Ever since he got back from Texas, he's been a total pain: he says "yes" in English whenever he can! He's really laying it on thick.

UN-BEAR-A-BLE!

Tom and I said farewell, and I went to Mrs. Joviol's class, my new homeroom. This year I found myself seated next to Nico (Nicolas Frilo, the new kid). At first glance he seems cool.

😊 And what luck! Naïs was sitting just in front of me. I was so happy . . . until she turned around and asked:

"Was that really you acting like a sea lion on the beach in Brittany?"

 She'd seen me! 😨

I became totally red and cursed 😠 Lisa and her stupid "Shrimp Splash" game! Fortunately, Mrs. Joviol began describing our schedule, and that diverted Naïs's attention. Raoul was seated near the back of the room. He'd fashioned a "blowgun" out of a pen and was shooting spitballs at the back of Chloé Dubuc's head, who—without realizing—was looking more and more like a grandma covered with foil at the hairdresser. 😄 Except one shot completely missed its target.

😮

The teacher scanned the class to find the culprit. Considering Chloé's head, it wasn't hard to guess that the pellet perpetrator was just behind her. The blowgun was confiscated, as well as the cowboy hat. I thought this punishment was too lenient. Personally, I would have opted for immediate and permanent expulsion.

MY STUPID SCHEDULE

	MONDAY	TUESDAY	WEDNESDAY	THURSDAY	FRIDAY
8:00	GERMAN Level 2 Mrs. Strauss	ENGLISH Level 1 Mr. Crazot	PE Mr. Ramoupoulos	TECHNOLOGY Mr. Cariou	MATH Mrs. Joviol
9:00	ENGLISH Level 1 Mr. Crazot	MUSIC Mr. Tuguet	PE Mr. Ramoupoulos	FRENCH Mr. Gaffard	ENGLISH Level 1 Mr. Crazot
10:00	FRENCH Mr. Gaffard	FRENCH Mr. Gaffard	MATH Mrs. Joviol	FRENCH Mr. Gaffard	FRENCH Mr. Gaffard
11:00	LIFE SKILLS Mrs. Ficelle		ENGLISH Level 1 Mr. Crazot	SOCIAL STUDIES Mrs. Gigolet	SOCIAL STUDIES Mrs. Gigolet
12:00					
1:30	SOCIAL STUDIES Mrs. Gigolet	MATH Mrs. Joviol		VISUAL ARTS Mrs. Manchon	
2:30	BIOLOGY Mrs. Le Clone	PHYSICS/ CHEMISTRY Mrs. Dupuis		GERMAN Level 2 Mrs. Strauss	
3:30		TECHNOLOGY Mr. Cariou		PE Mr. Ramoupoulos	
4:30				PE Mr. Ramoupoulos	
5:30					

41

My mom went to the back-to-school parents' night organized by Mrs. Joviol. Apparently, Mrs. Joviol spent most of the time talking about our future trip to England. 😎 She also explained to the parents that the main goal of seventh grade was to make us more INDEPENDENT. Specifically, she said that even if we didn't do our homework, there wouldn't be any punishment. . . . Sounds like a great idea to me! 😛 But the fun didn't last. Since my mom thought my schedule looked "light," she signed me up for another activity:

{ **READING PASSION CLUB**
Led by Françoise Toinou
Member: Max Cropin

You see, dear future human, I thought not being in Tom's class would AT LEAST mean everyone would leave me THE FLIP alone this year. . . . But ohhhh no! I'm not a big fan of reading, sure, but I *hate* the idea of joining a book club called "Reading Passion!"

Wednesday

Since the back-to-school meeting, I haven't done a single page of homework. I'm perfectly happy just taking notes in my Pietro planner. And then this morning, during English class, Mr. Crazot sent me to the board to correct a paragraph that we were supposed to have gone through at home the night before.

End result: I got a zero.

? Uhhh, I dunno!

───── CONCLUSION ─────

Teachers are first-rate tricksters. In front of the parents they're shaking in their boots and don't dare say a thing. But then they take it out on the "vulnerable"—like us students—and make our lives <u>HARD</u>.

Here I am, extra annoyed: not only do I have to do my homework but I'm also stuck in Reading Passion! 😎

Today was the club's first meeting. Mrs. Toinou is the president, but luckily she enlisted some retired ladies to help give us an "appetite for reading." That means I don't have to deal with HER directly. On the other hand, I'm with Mrs. Raymond, Naïs's grandma. And that puts extreme pressure on me. 😖 If I want any chance that ole Grandma Raymond will put in a good word with Naïs, I've got to look extremely smart. On the plus side, Raoul Kador 😀 isn't part of the club. And that, future human, is <u>a real</u> relief! 😛

All things considered, being in Reading Passion could be a REAL breath of fresh air in my life. The only other guy from my class who's in the club is the new student: Nico. 🙂 The first session of Reading Passion consisted of introducing ourselves and discussing THE book that "turned our existence upside down." I, for one, found that question a bit "premature." I'm still young, and I have PLENTY of time to find THE book that will change my life. Anyway, it took a lot of effort to search my memory. I vaguely remembered a book called *Tilulu and the Flute* from kindergarten, but it's nothing to brag about.

All of a sudden, I had a stroke of genius. I didn't just have one book title to share, but TWO! 🙂

My name is Max Cropin, and my favorite books are Zombieland Anthology: 1 and 2 and Extreme Excavator.

When Nico gave me a thumbs-up, I thought everyone was impressed and I was going to win brownie points with Naïs's grandma, but in fact . . . he was <u>the only one</u> to appreciate my literary taste. Everyone else just gave me strange looks.

If you want my opinion, it wasn't a success. . . .

Friday

I went back to Reading Passion, and Mrs. Toinou told us that we were going to participate in a "Readers' Choice Contest." How can I put this? . . . We all have to read ten books over the course of the year, write reports on them, and, at the end, vote for which one we liked the best . . . ten books!!! Do you understand? And real books, made of PAPER. If only they'd given us Nipads, I would have been way more motivated. Mrs. Raymond passed out the list, and, believe me future human, I was totally dismayed.

A Life of Nothing
Journey to the Edge of Midnight
Forgetting the Forgotten
Green and Yellow
Mrs. Racornie
Father Gorilla
Poachers Have a Heavy Hand
Sparkling Water Murders
The Deadly Flowers
Cannibal Burger

On the way home, Nico told me his mom signed him up for the reading club so he could "make some friends." But really, he's just like me—reading isn't one of his "priorities." Conclusion: We have to find a way to get out of this whole reading report deal. And as it happens, we bumped into Tom! 😊 Perfect timing.

Super Slug always has twelve billion good ideas in his pocket! We explained our ENORMOUS problem, and he immediately told us to go to the library and check out one of those *Qwik Notes* guides. Apparently, they summarize books so you DON'T have to read them, and they give some "analytical" blah blah so you can look really smart. Fantastic! These little books sound wicked cool. It's exactly what we need! For that matter, I also thought I'd seen a few copies of them in Marion's room.

I looked in Marion's room, but I couldn't get my hands on any copies of *Qwik Notes*. Mom must have sold them at the last garage sale. This morning, Nico and I went to the library and found EVERYTHING. We ran through the *Cannibal Burger* guide at top speed in fifteen minutes, and we decided to keep the copies of *Qwik Notes* until our next work session. I have the feeling that, if everything goes as planned, Naïs's grandma is finally going to recognize my brilliance, and soon she'll fall into my arms. Naïs, ehh? Not her grandma!

Last night, during dinner, my mom informed us all that she's decided to start doing YOGA. (··)

She signed up for a class on Tuesday nights. At first, I thought this development meant big trouble: making dinner on our own. Umm ... dear future human, I should point out that my dad doesn't know the first thing about cooking, as you'll soon understand! But two minutes later, I realized the benefit of this situation:

Who votes for Fastburger tonight?

I thought the vote would be unanimous, but guess what? My dad totally shot down my plans. He decided that, from now on, Tuesday night would be the perfect chance to finish ALL the "leftovers" in the fridge.

When I heard him rummaging around in the kitchen and humming, I got a bad feeling . . . and my intuition never fails me. When he proudly served us his "mixed salad," I nearly passed out.

I was really wishing we had a dog right about then. . . .

melon

sardines

noodles

oil

blue cheese

anchovies

pickles

hard-boiled eggs

Tuesday night again . . . week two of the mixed salad . . . It's become a joke with Marion and Lisa. We invented a food review guide called *Upchuck Weekly* 😱 and gave tonight's dinner five stars: cauliflower base, chicken nuggets, bell peppers, lentils, and a hint of mustard. When my mom came home from yoga class, she told me that Mrs. Raymond—Naïs's grandma—was also doing yoga. I wasn't too sure how to take the news. 😁 Apparently, she told my mom that Nico and I had really impressed her with our "analysis" of *Cannibal Burger* and that I seemed very "mature" for my age. 🥸 She even asked if I'd written the report all by myself. All in all, my mom seemed to find this very fishy. I ran up to my room and sent a text to Nico.

We agreed that I'd hide all the evidence likely to get us caught. Imagine if someone discovered our trick and we ended up in prison? So I decided to stash the books in my trash can until I could sneak them back to the library

Wednesday

Yesterday, I panicked too fast with the whole *Qwik Notes* thing. When I came home from school earlier, I discovered with horror that my trash can had been emptied! 😱 I told Nico right away. He didn't want to hear a word of it, but I was worried sick!

1. These books don't belong to me. I BORROWED them from the library. 😕
2. I need to figure out a way to replace them.
3. I'm totally broke. . . .

But this isn't my only problem.

4. My dad's concoctions are destroying my digestive tract.

5. Marion hasn't stopped wearing her leather pants now that it's fall. This morning we left together, and they made an irritating noise with every step.

6. And this wish bracelet won't break, even when I scrub it in the shower! If this goes on much longer, I'm going to end up without a hand.

With all of these worries, it's impossible for me to concentrate on my paper for *Poachers Have a Heavy Hand,* which is due Friday without mistakes . . . and <u>WITHOUT</u> the help of *Qwik Notes.*

😊 I flipped through the book *Children Soft as Pandas* to see if I could find a good relaxation exercise. I opened right to a page that suggested "visualizing" your body in a room, then in a city, then in the country, then above the earth, and the galaxy. . . . It made me seriously dizzy, and the fear of being an astronaut lost in the universe came back. 😵 I closed the book as fast as possible.

As for the reading report, I decided to just go by the book title. It's a well-known fact that every respectable author puts everything into the title of the book. 🤓

I decided to message Nico to pass on my tip, and then I got down to business.

Poachers Have a Heavy Hand

by Jason Humphrey

Synopsis by Maxime Cropin 🙂

This story is about mean poachers/serial killers who slaughter lots of rhinos in order to steal their horns.

But in the middle of the night, they're all bitten on the hand by a giant spider. Their hands swell up, they run away, and no one ever sees them again.

A remarkable work, rather well written, with suspense on every page. 😛

Now all I had to do was hope Mrs. Raymond never wanted to read the book either! 😐

Dear future human,

Guess what? Poachers Have a Heavy Hand isn't about rhinos AT ALL—it's about <u>crocodiles.</u> 🤐 The poachers were nice <u>"converts"</u> who were raising baby reptiles on a farm and organizing crocodile "petting zoos." In the end, Mylène, a young French volunteer helping them, apparently falls in love with Daniel, the toughest of the poachers. None of which has anything to do with the title of the book, so . . . I completely bombed my report. 🤐 Nico didn't fare much better. He'd written that the "poachers" were the name of a sports team that traveled the world to compete in weight-lifting competitions. Mrs. Raymond didn't seem to appreciate our "vivid imaginations." What a shame! And all of this is because someone took the liberty of touching <u>my trash can.</u> 😠

Sunday

It's already fall break, and believe me, future human, it isn't a moment too soon! Some time off might give me the chance to find solutions to my problems.

Objective: get off on the right foot after vacation. My priorities are:

- Avoid my dad's "mixed salad" torture.
- Replace the *Qwik Notes* at the library.
- Restore my image in Mrs. Raymond's eyes in order to seduce Naïs.

And for all of these,
I can see only ONE SOLUTION:

↓

make some money.

So earlier today, I offered to handle the grocery shopping and "menu development" for my parents, in exchange for a small raise in allowance. My parents thought this was an EXCELLENT idea: it would be the perfect occasion for me to become more "independent." Most importantly, this will help me replace the books at the library and give me control over the leftovers.

Monday

Dear future human,

I called up Tom and Nico today. Lucky me—they hadn't gone on vacation either! So they were super motivated to go to the grocery store with me. 😊 I thought long and hard about my list in order to group foods that went TOGETHER.

hamburger + French fries

chicken nuggets + mac & cheese

hot dogs + potato chips

You'll notice that at no point did I ever mention __fish.__ And there's a good reason for that. Have I already told you the story about Bullotin? Bullotin was my goldfish.

😊

I won him in a game against Martin Picard at the school carnival when I was in first grade. I was so proud to have a pet. But one morning, I woke up and Bullotin was floating in his bowl. I called my dad to show him how well Bullotin could do the backstroke, but he told me to go brush my teeth. When I came back to my room, the bowl had disappeared.

Dad told me my fish had left to go to the Olympic Games on the other side of the world and that he wouldn't be coming back. I was really impressed: Bullotin had the spirit of a champion. I was so excited to tell the whole school about his adventure.

Except when I came back home from school, the first thing that I did was go to the bathroom. When I looked into the toilet bowl, I had the shock of my life!

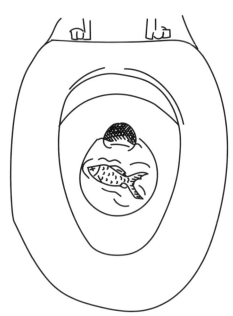

Dear future human, suffice it to say that this traumatic experience called for three sessions with a "shrink," and ever since then I refuse to eat fish. 😝

At the supermarket, Tom, Nico, and I noticed that there was a "promotional activity" for a new fruit juice. Someone dressed up as a monkey was giving out small paper cups of banana juice to shoppers. We went to go and see the monkey . . . well, I guess . . . the person dressed up as a monkey. 🐵

Get this: it was Philippe, my old babysitter! He recognized me right away. He told us that he was developing a new brand of juice that was "100% healthy and organic." 😄

We didn't really understand all of his explanations, but it's clear he had every intention of becoming RICH! But to tell you the truth, that didn't shock me at all. Back in the day, Philippe already had "the stuff" to be a businessman. When he would come to babysit us, we'd already taken our bath and dinner was ready. He didn't have to do ANYTHING ELSE except to say two things:

"Yum! Yum!" and "Bedtime!" Then he'd plop down in front of the TV until my parents came home and collect his $60.

Wednesday

My plan is working wonderfully! It's been almost two weeks since I started getting the groceries and managing meals. Since then, Dad's "leftover innovations" are a thing of the past! With all of his work at S Inc., my dad has permanently given up the meal planning. He even seems delighted with my "gourmet" specials.

And if my math is right, I've earned almost $55, which has helped me buy new copies of *Qwik Notes* for the library. Pshh!! To think, I could have bought *Dogs of Hell* with all of that money.

 Dear future human,

You can choose to believe me or not, but all of the copies of *Qwik Notes* from the library reappeared on my desk as if by magic! 😮 As I was sitting there, absolutely astonished, my mom came in my room. I realized that <u>she</u> had tricked me! My mom explained that she'd wanted to show me how bad it was to cheat, but since I'd proven myself to be very "mature," she'd decided to return the guides if I promised to go exchange them tomorrow for the 〔real〕books assigned for Reading Passion.

Mom, I love you, but I was almost in DEEP doo-doo because of <u>YOU</u>! Not to mention the fact that I now have TWO copies of *Qwik Notes*!

Friday

I went and returned my copies of *Qwik Notes* to the bookstore and took the others back to the library, where I spent most of the day with Nico working on the papers for Reading Passion. Fortunately, I know that real readers actually "skim"—and believe me, that's exactly what we did. 😊 We were done around 3:00 p.m. It's crazy how much I'm putting into a silly reading club! 😄

Afterward, Nico and I went for a walk. Since he just moved here, I told him about all of my adventures from last year. Nico comes from the south of France. He told me that his dad died in a car accident. That really moved me. . . . 🙁 His mom was transferred around here this year, which is how he ended up at our school.

We had a lot of stuff to share: he loves trail mix, American basketball (especially LeBron James),  and video games. He's an astronomy buff and a fan of the TV show *Middle School Madness*. And the worst present he's ever received is doughnut slippers for his eighth birthday. The slippers were so huge that he tripped and broke a leg! I couldn't stop myself from laughing, and neither could he. This dude is pretty cool!

Monday

One day back in school, and I've already had enough! Today in science, Mrs. Le Clone told us we were going to go over a sensitive subject: puberty and reproduction. Needless to say, that was all it took for the whole class to break out in laughter. 😆 Then the teacher announced that she was going to show us a video. 😐

As for me, I'm an expert on the question of where babies come from. 😉 When I was eight, my dad took me aside and got out a book that had to have been in our family for at least five generations.

The Seeds of Love

I think my parents were just paranoid that Marion would spill the beans . . . like she always does. Luckily this discussion didn't happen when my dad was learning Russian, or I would've been completely lost.

At least something juicy was FINALLY going down at school. The last REAL questions I'd been wondering about would be answered once and for all. Questions like: What do "mosquito bites" have to do with girls' chests? In order to be a real man, do you have to know how to raise only one eyebrow instead of both? How do you get a deep and masculine voice? If you put deodorant on your cheeks, does that make your beard grow faster? Mrs. Le Clone started the video and then turned out the lights and demanded complete silence.

I used this as an opportunity to change seats and slide in next to Naïs. This documentary was <u>THE CHANCE OF A LIFETIME</u> to get closer to her. And—if I could muster the courage—I would even try to hold her hand at exactly the most romantic moment.

The video started, and suddenly the title of the documentary came on the screen:

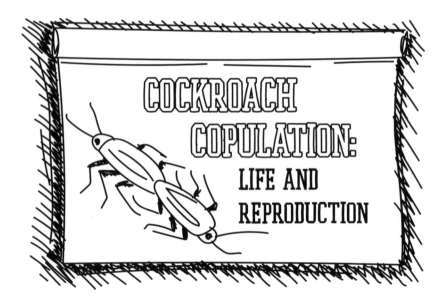

COCKROACH COPULATION: LIFE AND REPRODUCTION

Wednesday

Since seventh grade has been nothing but a string of disappointments so far, I've decided to put all my hopes into a much more spectacular project. Why? For three simple reasons:

1. To quit worrying about school (thanks to reason #3).
2. To impress Naïs.
3. To get <u>RICH.</u>

And I've given it some thought. If I want to "charm" Naïs, I need to become someone important . . .

ASAP!

Everyone knows that, in movies, girls are always attracted to the successful guys with ambition.

Well, well, dear future human, my genius brain had no trouble sprouting a totally awesome idea! 😊 I am going to create A BRAND that will be called I.A.G. as in . . . IT'S ALL GOOD! It'll be just like Philippe, my old babysitter, and his innovative banana juice! My plan is to create T-shirts and baseball caps with graffiti designs.

So this afternoon I got together with Nico and that ole slug Tom to explain my project. Jackpot! They wanted in. Tom will be the designer, Nico will be the communication director, and I'll be the project director. Pretty cool, huh?

You may now address me by my formal title, Professor Maestro MAXimum (dolla billz) Bossman.

I had a TERRIBLE weekend 😠 Yesterday, my parents decided that we needed to spend more time together as a family. So out of the blue, they took us to a little amusement park called Game Yard—but it was a total fiasco! I was stuck in the "Cursed Labyrinth" for <u>two hours.</u> My parents kept waving at me frantically from above to tell me which way to go, but I didn't understand a thing. I was going in circles for what felt like an eternity, constantly bumping into the walls. Finally, they went and got one of the supervisors to lead me to the exit.

Then a huge bulldog took a bite out of Lisa's cotton candy. She started wailing until we finally went home.

I miss you, mon amour! Kisses from Brittany 🖤🖤🖤

And to top it all off, my parents stumbled on Marion's phone, where they found some compromising texts. 😶

And so they immediately confiscated her phone, and my dad gave her a lecture about how Tristan Le Bouzec was FAR TOO OLD for her. 😷

Ever since then, she's been in a horrible mood! She's acting like she has a broken heart because of my parents' cruelty, but if you ask me, dear future human, she's really just obsessed with her phone. 😖

My brand project isn't moving forward at all. 😕 Tom was supposed to show me "prototypes," but I haven't seen squat, and that wimp has been MIA since Friday. I've gone to the secret passage a few times to wait for him, but he hasn't shown up. Nico is still thinking about a "media strategy," but we have to hurry up or someone might steal my idea.

In other news, right now at school it's all the rage to write little notes in each other's planners. It's the perfect way for me to slip Naïs a message that's both "original" and "poetic." 😜 🌼 And believe me, dear future human, I am a far more romantic writer than Tristan Le Bouzec. 😍

Naïs,

I'm happy to be in class with YOU.

I hope you feel the same way TOO.

Max

Draft

But this <u>moron Raoul</u> went ALL OUT. He practically wrote "I love you" in all of the girls' planners!

As for the boys, they were entitled to a much more . . . special treatment: he stuck his old chewed-up gum in all of our planners!

A little while back, my mom decided to start waking up at six in the morning. She's convinced that getting up before sunrise is <u>THE</u> secret to "becoming one's best self." Personally, I don't share my mother's new obsession. A teenager needs lots of sleep; it's proven science! And it's precisely because of this fact that this morning I slept in, was super late, and didn't have a choice:

But at the end of the day, there was a message on the front gate of school that forced me to make a drastic decision: NEVER AGAIN am I going to ask an adult for help.

Reminder

Appropriate clothing is required at all times while at school. This applies to students AS WELL AS TO PARENTS. Thank you for not wearing pajamas.

The Principal

I've just discovered something: Tom has been out of touch recently because he's spending A LOT OF TIME with Célia. Here's what happened. As I was leaving school, I completely stumbled upon them kissing on the street corner.  Frankly, it wasn't a pretty sight to see!

Since then he seems to be floating on cloud nine. How could that snail double-cross me like this?

Tom . . .
It's All Good?
Forgetting
anything???

Wednesday

So Tom and Célia are officially in love, and it's totally messing with my head. Yesterday morning, there was no one at the secret passage. They came to school hand in hand, and they spent all of recess together.

Dear future human, I can already hear you saying I'm jealous. Well . . . you're not wrong. I'd be pretty happy if Naïs fell in love with me. Why does it always feel like good things only happen to other people?

Thankfully, I wasn't all alone. In the lunchroom, Nico told me that he'd just come up with our brand logo:

LOGO

It was a terrific idea, and it even made me smile again! 🙂 Last night I suddenly decided to send a text to Tom and Nico for an emergency meeting. <u>A little bit of pressure and everything will be in order!</u> Dear future human, I think I've already got the right stuff to be a major "business executive."

This afternoon, Tom began sketching designs for our collection, and the results were killer. Yellow heads with big smiles—it was awesome. 🙂🙂🙂🙂🙂🙂 Meanwhile, Nico told me that he had another idea: since he's enrolled at the YMCA, he'd heard that there was a gardening activity planned before Christmas with a group of old folks from the nursing home, Pleasant Gardens. He suggested that all three of us sign up for it with the GOAL of organizing an IAG presale there. I thought that was brilliant! 😁

Friday

Presto! We enrolled in the old folks' activity without any problem. So far, I want to say, It's All Good! LOL 😄 Obviously, you can bet we didn't tell them we were going to participate just so we could advertise our brand. Still, the activity seemed kinda cool: gardening on the main grounds of the retirement home and having a snack with the seniors. The other good news is that since this summer, Mrs. Quinion, my old neighbor, has been living at Pleasant Gardens. She's the perfect person to PULL STRINGS for us! 😌 Like I said—I already have the spirit of a CEO! 😎

Dow Jones? Chow Jones!

When I told my mom about all this, she said I'm "improving myself by the day." I definitely won't be the one to tell her otherwise. 🙂

Monday

Tom told Célia about how we were going to Pleasant Gardens to join their outing. She apparently passed this on to Naïs, who seemed really impressed with our generosity. 😊 This made me realize Tom and Célia could be a serious asset in my efforts to charm Naïs. 🤭 But I also had to draft contracts for Tom and Nico with a "confidentiality clause."

Numero uno, if our idea got out, Raoul or one of his losers could steal it.

Numero two-no, I wouldn't want Naïs to discover our "business" and think I'm just some kind of self-serving person. 😐

OFFICIAL

IAG

I _____
I swear to keep the IAG project top secret.

Spit here

Today was the big day! Time for our visit to Pleasant Gardens. Tom, Nico, and I were totally ready. I'd practiced some sales techniques from Nico. I'd even gone back to several relaxation exercises from *Children Soft as Pandas*,  in case the jitters prevented me from being convincing. And I have to admit that Tom did a really good job. We three make a nice team!

Tada!

IAG— clothes that make you look all good!

So after school, we took the bus to the retirement home. Guess who came along with the group? <u>Ramoupoulos, the PE teacher!</u> Unlike last year, no one was waiting for us at the entrance, and we stood there forever till someone opened the gate for us. I wanted to get back on the bus, but it had already left.

(Just between us, I always wonder what the bus drivers are up to while we're on field trips.)

We had to walk all the way from the gate to the building. Ramoupoulos got it in his head to make us jog the whole way, so I arrived at the front door out of breath, red, and covered in sweat.

My very first action after becoming a confirmed businessman will be hiring a chauffeur!

What happened next, dear future human, was not great. . . . It started to rain cats and dogs, so much that the gardening was canceled. So then half of the old folks decided to snooze in their rooms. We wound up shut away in a projection room, watching a horribly boring documentary about illness prevention. I looked around me, and I didn't see any of the people who I sang "Hope and Life" in front of last year. I didn't even see Mrs. Quinion, who could've saved me from this whole situation. At one point, Nico spotted a little old lady who seemed nice. He was elbowing me to join him and go see her. But before we got up, she fell asleep . . .

and she was followed close behind by Ramoupoulos, who started snoring louder than half of the old folks combined!

This went on for two hours!

Yuck!

Not to mention the snack afterword didn't exactly meet our expectations . . .

Ultra-dry raisin fruitcake

Eventually, Ramoupoulos told us that the bus had arrived—and not a moment too soon. On the way home, I was asking myself if I should just switch my career path to school bus driver.

This morning, Tom, Nico, and I "debriefed" between classes. Debrief is a term my dad often uses when he comes back from S Inc. And I'm sure Philippe, my old babysitter, debriefs all the time for his juice business.

We'd failed at the whole IAG presale, but we'd figured out the elderly are not the ideal clientele for our products.

Howdy-do, youngsters!

CONCLUSION:
WE'RE SNAPPING BACK, MOVING ON, AND KEEPING IT UP!

Friday

This morning, in the middle of social studies with Mrs. Gigolet, the principal came to our class. He informed us that a new student would be arriving in January.

He tormented us with an entire speech on the "spirit of solidarity" we'll need to demonstrate, because according to him, the new student is <u>disabled.</u>

It's Christmas, and you are never going to guess what was waiting for me under the tree: *Dogs of Hell*! I'd totally forgotten about the advertisement at Grandpa Joff and Grandma Ragny's house this summer, and they'd found the little piece of paper rolled into a ball at the very end of the backyard. What's funny is that they had the amazing idea to give it to me, but they had no clue it was <u>THE game I'd been dreaming about for the past six months!</u> I think my luck is finally turning around. 😄

As for my present ideas, I didn't have to think too hard. As you know, I'm the gift-giving champion!

My parents were easiest—I gave them a present in the form of "stocks." 😖

0.0001% IN I.A.G.

0.0001% IN I.A.G.

0.0001% IN I.A.G.

0.0001% IN I.A.G.

0.0001% IN I.A.G.

0.0001% IN I.A.G.

0.0001% IN I.A.G.

0.0001% IN I.A.G.

0.0001% IN I.A.G.

0.0001% IN I.A.G.

Marion is way harder to buy for. Usually, she doesn't like any of her presents and has to exchange them.

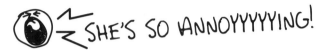 SHE'S SO ANNOYYYYYYING!

I knew my parents had bought her a rainbow sweater with huge stripes. I also knew she wouldn't like it one bit, so it occurred to me to dig up the receipt. I made her a card, and it didn't cost me a penny:

SWEATERS
GALORE
12 Street St.
TEL: (014) 033-7896
FAX: (014) 023-7788
12000 SMILEY
....
RNBW SWEATER
TOTAL _____
....

If it's out of style
If you don't like presents
If it's too short
If it itches
If it's ugly
If the size doesn't work
If the zipper pinches
If the style doesn't work
If the color doesn't work
If it smells bad
If it's too gangsta, etc.

For Lisa, I remembered the website www.
stupidpresents.com. It's the site my whole family
used to make that goody bag for my birthday.
And I found THE perfect gift for my little
sister.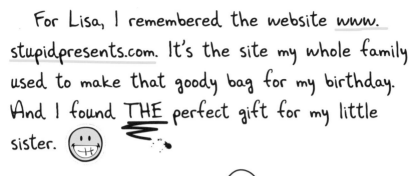

I know my presents are going to be a total
home run. Merry Christmas, dear future human!

Saturday

Dear future human,

Between Christmas and the New Year, Marion and Lisa left for a few days to see Grandpa Joff and Grandma Ragny in Brittany. Well, if we're being honest, Marion really went to see Tristan Le Bouzec. 😊 Dad and Mom had asked Grandpa and Grandma to "keep an eye on them," but I don't think they'll really follow orders. . . .

As for me, I decided to stay here and make some progress on IAG. I mainly saw only Nico—Tom was apparently too busy with Célia. I sent him a bunch of texts, but each time he told me he was going to the movies or to the library or to a dance or to knitting club. . . . Célia this, Célia that, Célia blah blah blah. 😠 Plus I saw that Fastburger just launched a new advertising campaign for Valentine's Day. The gist of it was to hug or kiss at the register in order to get their "Enormo Fastburger."

A GOLDEN opportunity to invite Naïs! 😊

But two days later I was passing in front of
Fastburger, and I found out that old slug had
betrayed me **YET AGAIN.**

I'm starting to think that my friendship
with Tom is fading. Girls are cool and all, but
when one tries to get between two dudes, it's
pretty much hopeless.

Luckily, Nico and I are getting somewhere. He showed me lots of other faces he invented for our brand: one <u>crying from laughing</u>, one <u>green with fright</u>, some that <u>aren't happy</u>,  others <u>sticking out their tongues</u>. . . .

I helped him scribble out the faces so Tom could draw them later . . . when His Majesty is finally AVAILABLE, that is. Like I already said, we decided to make shirts and baseball hats.

And the good news is that Nico's mom works at a company that might be able to print them. We only have to convince her to help. This guy has loads of good ideas!

Nico and I also played *Dogs of Hell* (maybe a bit too much), and I have to say he's super good.

We also watched two whole seasons of *Middle School Madness*. It's a great show about some teenagers who start a rock band. They practice in a garage and suddenly become famous thanks to a clip posted on Zikpoint, a video-hosting site.

My parents and I went to visit Mimi yesterday to wish her a happy New Year. I haven't had the chance to tell you much about her, but Mimi is one of a kind. She's my dad's mom.

We don't see her that often, but Dad calls her the "Dinosaur": she is really old and almost as vicious as a T. rex. 😁 Her house always smells like good coffee, because she lives on the second floor right above an "itsy-bitsy café," as she likes to say. When I grow up, I'm going to drink gallons of coffee . . . like a real businessman. 😎

🏠 When you enter, you have to walk down a really dark hallway before coming to a room that she uses for a little bit of everything: living room, kitchen, and even bedroom. Every time we visit, this hallway seems never-ending, because Mimi walks super slow! 😠 But the strangest thing is that she's always seated in the exact same armchair, which is completely deformed. If you want my opinion, it's taken on the shape of her butt after all those years of sitting on it. 😝 I'm always worried the chair will break, Mimi will fall through it, and she'll end up in the coffee shop below. 😱

My mom says Mimi isn't very pleasant and she has a "sharp tongue." That totally freaked me out when I was five years old. One time, I asked Mimi to stick out her tongue, which caused a big mess.

Mom, you're wrong. Mimi doesn't have a sharp tongue.

Mimi always thinks Marion wears too much makeup, Lisa is too skinny, and my parents work too much. But me? She adores me! You see, I'm the family's only "heir." Thanks to yours truly, the looooooong line of Cropins is sure to continue! I should also admit that I have a trick: each year, I draw a picture for her. And believe me, I don't have to work too hard.

Mimi and Max

Mimi has them all in a big stack on her counter, because she appreciates all my "little acts of kindness." 🙂 Anyway, she spent the whole visit criticizing our family. And Dad and Mom spent the whole visit nodding their heads and saying, "Ah! Oh! Yes? Really?" Both of them seemed really tense. 😁 But above all, Mimi has a <u>strange device</u> in her ear, which makes this loud, awful whistle. It's like her ear is superhuman—even bionic. And since she leaves the TV on, it's a total cacophony. 😮 It's impossible to stay in that room for more than ten minutes. So I went to walk around the apartment and the "real" living room, which is used only for "special occasions."

When no one's around, it feels like some kind of haunted museum. 👻 It's all dark and super creepy. 😬 There are also lots of framed photos of people I don't know. Except . . . I noticed that one of them was <u>Auntie Yum Yum.</u> 😮 I'd totally forgotten about her! It's been forever since I last saw her. Want to know why we call her that? It's because when Mimi was still able to organize family get-togethers, Aunt Yum Yum was always first in line to eat. 😵 I think that she only came for the food. And once she was in the front, she would always sing, "Yum, yum, yum," with her plate in hand. We'd make fun of her every time, and it became a family joke.

Before we left, Mimi gave me an envelope and said it was for me alone. She said my sisters simply had to come and see her if they wanted the same thing. 😛

<u>BURN!</u>

Then she gave my parents a box of chocolates, but inside, half of the chocolates were already gone.

Besides all that, during break I took advantage of the time to sift through our basement. I

always unearth stuff Mom and Dad have forgotten about. Like . . . these REALLY strange pictures of them from when they were "young."

Another time, I ran across a pacifier collection, and there was no mistaking who they belonged to.

In that box, I also found fake cardboard tokens that my mom had made. On them was written:

> 1 NIGHT-NIGHT WITHOUT PACIFIER = 1 POINT
> 5 POINTS = 1 PRESENT

First, I'd just made one heck of a discovery: Marion used to have a pacifier!!! RI-DI-CU-LOUS

Second, I realized that, on the topic of presents, she had a considerable head start on me!

Third, this intel could prove to be extremely useful in months or years to come, if you know what I mean!

This time around, I ended up with a faux-fur blanket as a result of my subterranean expedition. I have no idea who could've possibly owned such a treasure, but since it's freezing cold right now, it seemed perfect! I brought the blanket upstairs, and every night since I've curled up with it to watch TV.

Dear future human,

Monday

I'm back in school, and guess what: there were quite a few changes to accommodate the "disabled" student, who the principal talked to us about before vacation. 😮 In fact, there are access ramps <u>EVERYWHERE:</u> in front of the lunchroom, the gym, and the computer room. A bathroom two times bigger than the others was even put in, but we aren't allowed to use it. 🙁 The classes were even rearranged so that every room for our class is on the first floor.

So the disabled student arrived this morning, and it's . . . A GIRL! 👧 She's seated next to Naïs, so almost in front of me. Her name is Lena. "Disabled" seemed a bit vague to me, so I had imagined all sorts of horrible things before she got here.

All of this was because one day I read lots of weird things online about rare diseases: people covered with hair or pustules. . . . I even heard some people can pass out if they laugh too hard—it's called "laughter-induced syncope."

It's really annoying if someone tells you a good joke.

What's the purpose of goose bumps? To keep the geese from speeding!

As for Lena, except for the fact she's in a wheelchair, it's not at all obvious that she has a "problem." Truthfully, I think she's quite pretty—but NOT as pretty as Naïs.

The entire time in French class, Nico was totally hypnotized. But I heard that big idiot Raoul say, "Looks like we've got an old granny!" I found that to be extremely mean.

Tonight during dinner, after I told my family about Lena's arrival, Lisa kept asking me a million questions about disabled people. The subject seemed to really interest her! In other news, ever since I found that fuzzy blanket, Marion's started to sit at the other end of the couch, and it ANNOYYYYYS me so much!

Monday

This morning, something funny happened in German class. We were supposed to memorize the German alphabet during winter break. Mrs. Strauss asked if there were any volunteers to recite it by singing the song we learned. I raised my hand without any hesitation: it was the perfect chance to snag a good grade. I cleared my throat and tried to muster my most beautiful voice (to impress Naïs).

I did pretty well, given that I was put on the spot, and I got a 20/20! Since there were no more volunteers, Mrs. Strauss quizzed Raoul. But this dimwit still had bubble gum in his mouth. In his haste, he tried to throw it over his shoulder, but the sticky glob fell back down . . . on his head!

Very, very bad idea! The teacher tried to stop him right away, but it was too late. We spent the rest of class watching Mrs. Strauss try to remove the globs of gum tangled in his hair. 😝 She didn't make much progress, so she sent him to the nurse. When he came back, he had a huge bald spot in the middle of his head. What a DISASTER! The nurse had to shave his head in order to get out all of the bubble gum.

Thursday

We started endurance training again with Mr. Ramoupoulos in PE. It is everything I feared—and more.  Apparently "endurance" means ten laps WITHOUT STOPPING: pure torture for an intellectual such as myself!  I felt like I was going to die . . . and that was just after the warm-up! What's more, I thought that after welcoming a student in a wheelchair, this practice was totally inappropriate because Lena couldn't participate.  I also realized that Raoul's bald patch gave him a competitive edge. After all, plenty of athletes shave their hair so they can be more aerodynamic. So that meant Raoul could probably pass us all! And he'd also be faster since the teachers made him take off the cowboy hat he was wearing to cover up his chrome dome.

Anyway, we took our places on the starting line, Ramoupoulos blew the whistle, and we were off. After two minutes, though, he told us to come back to the starting line because <u>Inès</u> and <u>Fatiha</u> had done something dumb:

The false start had already sucked up at least 68% of my energy. Thankfully, Nico ran next to me, and he suggested we keep Ramoupoulos in our sights so we could slow down and walk as soon as he wasn't looking. This trick proved to be quite effective— especially when, after two laps, Louison Toinou barfed while running past Ramoupoulos.

The teacher was too busy cleaning to keep track of us, so Nico and I walked calmly until the end of the run. Then we bragged about finishing the five laps, which actually would have been a record for me.

I walked home with Tom this afternoon. It'd been ages since the last time we'd done that. We talked about our brand, the new designs that Nico'd come up with, and the products that we wanted to develop. I was afraid that this wimp would tell me he wanted out of our adventure, but not at all. He was still ready to move forward with it and promised to come over to my house next Wednesday. I'd heard that Célia, Naïs, and Lena were going to spend that afternoon with "just the girls" . . . which explains why Tom will finally be FREE!

Besides that, I'm starting to think my blanket is losing its effectiveness because of Marion. . . .

She is so
ANNOYYYYYYING!

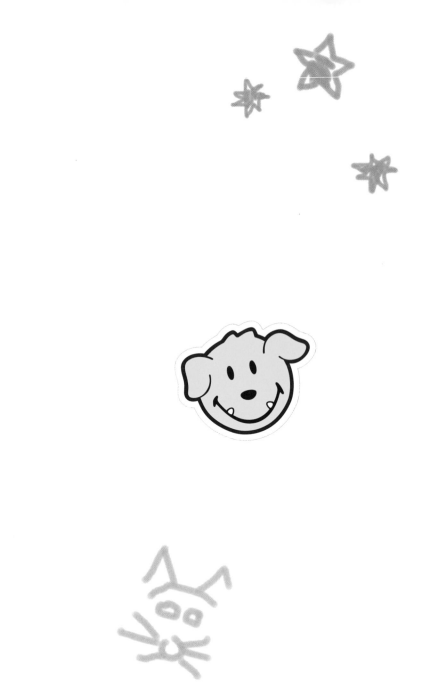

A lot happened this afternoon for our brand. Nico, Tom, and I shut ourselves up in my room, and I made sure no one would enter . . . especially Marion and Lisa.

We showed Tom the first drafts of the faces that we had scribbled with Nico's ideas. He thought they were sick. 🙂 Since he'd brought his spray cans and markers, he redesigned them in his own style. I even found an old plain T-shirt that we could try a stencil on. The result was honestly pretty good 🙂 Seeing it gave Nico an idea: we could make a video and post it online to make a name for ourselves, kind of like in *Middle School Madness*.

I remembered that my parents had an old video camera in the basement and went to go find it. We had to wait quite a while for that thing to finish charging, but sure enough it still worked! Except the tape inside wasn't exactly recent. . . . It was a video of me at seven or eight years old! On the screen, I was wearing a baseball hat backward, and I was belting out a song I'd made up. It was called "The Biker Bears." One look and you could tell my style wasn't all that great at the time.

Since I didn't really know how the camera worked, it took me forever to find the stop button. It was too late! Tom and Nico had seen it all, and they exploded with laughter. The shame! 😟 Well, I guess the fact that this video was forgotten in the basement meant it wasn't of interest to ANYONE. And while I'm still completely anonymous, I must remove any trace of my ridiculous nonsense. I rewound that tape so we could record our video over it. 😫

We created an entire set behind us with our brand logo and the figures Nico invented. We positioned the camera so you could see all three of us in front of the backdrop, then I pressed RECORD. I explained the concept of the brand, Tom did some "live" graffiti, and Nico presented the products that would soon be "available for sale."

I was worried it looked a little amateurish because we didn't have any real models yet, but in two takes it was a wrap. We decided Nico would post the video, since he knows the most about social media and he's the only one who has his own computer.

Then he shared some good news with us: he'd talked with his mom about our project, and she'd decided to supply us with about a hundred T-shirts and hats. That gave me a much-needed boost after the whole home video incident! Finally, our plans were materializing for REAL! I've got to say—I see nothing but glory, success, and fame in my future!

My parents came home, and Nico and Tom left. After dinner, I asked my mom if I could use the computer for just five minutes so I could check out our video online.

I went to NewTube and discovered that our "promotional" film was a total fiasco. On the screen everything was OK, but <u>the sound was all messed up.</u>

When I got to Broadway,

YEAH!

The biker bears clawed me!

HEY! . . .

Not the slightest bit amusing, if you ask me! I sent a text to Nico to alert him to the emergency so he could <u>delete every</u> trace of this agonizing failure from the internet. . . .

I was planning on a nice, chill night on the sofa, but the furry blanket was missing . . . along with Marion!

This morning in Life Skills class, Mrs. Ficelle took the whole hour to remind us of the importance of respecting people with disabilities and, more specifically, of respecting Lena. (☺) She told us that about 15% of the world's population lives with a disability, but most of them are able to overcome adversity with more strength than people who are considered "ordinary." Can you imagine, future human? <u>That's crazy!</u> (☺) I never would've thought it was that many people! Mrs. Ficelle congratulated the students who'd welcomed Lena, but she also told us that certain people at school had nicknamed her "Iron Queen," (☺) which according to her is completely unacceptable behavior. (☹)

Personally, I thought that sounded a little like a superhero name. But when I saw that moron Raoul shoot a spitball on Mathis's head, I realized exactly WHO, once again, had come up with this tasteless joke.

DOUBLE-DOG DARE

THE WORST CHALLENGES (FOR RAOUL)

Drink a shot of vinegar. *Fail!*

Big idiot! Count all of your hair.

Calculate every decimal of pi.

Snort pepper. *Chicken*

Troll Put thirty marshmallows in your mouth.

Sneeze with your eyes open.

Tickle yourself. *Loser!*

Write "I should not make fun of others" 10,000 times. With only one pencil and no sharpener.

Lick your elbow. *Not even possible!*

Be a decent person for an entire week. *No way!*

132

Then Mrs. Ficelle gave Lena the floor, and she told us her story. She was hit by a car when she was six years old.  That's how she lost the use of her legs. The class was dead silent, but then she reassured us: "OK, I can never jump on a trampoline, but other than that I'm good—it's all good." At the end she added something that really stuck with us.

The real handicap is being stared at.

I don't know why, but during class Nico seemed deep in thought. Afterward, he totally disappeared in the hallway. I racked my brain to figure out what I could've done wrong. Was it because of the screwed-up video?

After school I could only find Tom and Célia, and we all walked home together. Célia couldn't stop talking about Lena. Célia and Naïs have become really close friends with her. That didn't surprise me about Naïs . . . she's so pretty and openhearted! 😉 I told them about Life Skills, the rumor about the terrible nickname given to Lena (by Raoul or Mathis), and her accident. They seemed really impressed by Lena's courage. 🙂

When I got home, no one was there, and the house was completely dark. And due to the whole Nico disappearance thing, I felt a little bit lonely. 😦

So since I needed something comforting, I went looking for MY fuzzy blanket! I hurried straight to Marion's room, and, just as I suspected, I found the fur comforter on HER bed! And because that blanket belongs to ME, I reclaimed it. 😠 I wanted to take the opportunity to rummage around in her things, but Marion came home at EXACTLY that moment! And guess what she was wearing? <u>My dad's old patched jacket!</u> If she didn't give me back my "pelt," I was going to tell on her. But in the end, I didn't even have to negotiate for anything. 😁

This morning, Tom tagged the wall of the secret passage.

Nico was absent again yesterday, but I was happy to see him back today. 😛 While we were running in PE, he told me that since Mrs. Ficelle's class, he'd been doing a lot of thinking about Lena and about disability in general. As a result, he'd come up with an idea, but he didn't know if I'd be into it. I was <u>ALL</u> ears. Basically, he said, <u>"What if our business became more like a charity?"</u> All of the stuff with Lena had reminded him of his dad. If he had survived the car crash and found himself in a wheelchair, Nico was certain his dad would've loved for us to fight for this cause. Then he told me that he'd signed up with an organization called Welcoming Wheelchairs, and he'd learned they were looking for money to train service dogs for disabled people.

Those pooches can do all kinds of AWESOM
stuff: <u>pick up</u> things, <u>turn on</u> the lights, <u>open</u>
doors, <u>press</u> elevator buttons, and even <u>bark</u> on
command.

My mind started racing at full speed.

I said: GREAT IDEA! 😉

This would be an UNPARALLELED
opportunity to impress the ladies . . . and do
something good for others, of course! 😍

ENORMOUS NEWS!!! I got a text from Naïs. She's having a birthday party two weeks from Saturday, and guess what? Yes! She invited me.

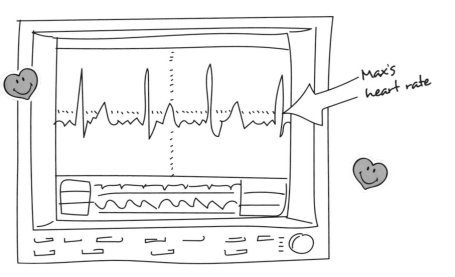

Max's heart rate

Hmm, well, give me a second to think about it . . . Umm, sure . . . that should work. I don't have too much planned for that night.

I'm going to wait until tomorrow to ask my mom. After her yoga class, she'll be A LOT more relaxed and likely to say YES.

Wednesday

Jackpot! Yesterday, Mom said YES to Naïs's party. 😊 And she came home from work today with a bag: she bought me new threads so I can look "presentable" for Mrs. Raymond. I thanked her and then stuffed the bag in my dresser before going to snuggle with my "fur" blanket. 😸

Dear future human,

I spent the entire afternoon looking for a present for Naïs. I should've started way earlier, because, guess what, figuring out what to give a girl in the twenty-first century isn't easy! 😜 Rule number one of the *Comprehensive Guide to Romance*: <u>find out</u> what your crush likes from her friends! Thankfully, there's a gift shop downtown where they sell all sorts of gizmos. And believe it or not, but today is Valentine's Day, so I found THE perfect gift.

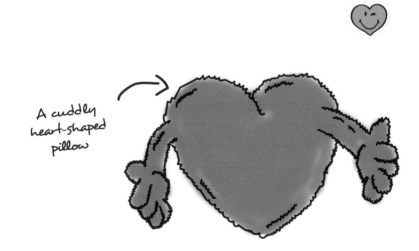

A cuddly heart-shaped pillow

And in the zipper, I had the brilliant idea to slide in a poem that rhymed with Naïs.

Naïs ♡

There's something inside me I need
to release:

My affections are for you—and daily increase.

My heart keeps on growing, it's almost obese.

But nevertheless it is slave to caprice.

Please tell me you love me and grant
my soul peace!

From: Max, your secret admirer
♡

So whatcha think? Not too shabby, eh?
Tonight's the BIG NIGHT, and I'm ready to
sweep Naïs off her feet!

The day after Naïs's party . . . How can I put this? . . . The night didn't start out so well, because when I tried on the clothes my mom had bought me, I quickly realized they weren't gonna work. 😑

T-shirt of a "nerdy" outfit

This was a total catastrophe, because it was already 5:30 p.m., and the party was starting thirty minutes later. ☹️ I would've loved to sneak down to Marion's room and get my hands on that old patched jacket of my dad's. I know I would've looked totally fly, 😎 but it was too late. I rifled through my closet and found the _IAG_ shirt that we'd made with the stencil. 😁

It was the only wearable thing I had on hand, so I put it on, threw a sweatshirt over it, slid my gift in my backpack, and left. Mom tried to corner me at the door and see if I was "handsome." But I managed to slip away quickly because I was already super late. 😁

When I arrived, there was a note for the neighbors taped to their doorbell, but someone had changed the words a little:

We are having a ~~little party~~ huge rager for ~~my granddaughter's birthday~~ that's gonna be totally wicked!

It's possible that there might be ~~a little bit of noise~~ hella noise!

Please don't excuse us for any disturbance.

For starters, we're calling the shots!

Sincerely, your neighbor ~~Danièle Raymond~~ the grouch on the fourth floor

I was sure <u>Raoul</u> or one of his goons had already been here. 😞 And I wasn't wrong. Right when I walked in, I bumped into Damien‼️ Chico—who was holding something strange in his hand. He said it was an "energy drink" and we ALL had to try it or otherwise we'd be "sissies." Basically, this idiot wanted to poison us! 👹 I had to put a stop to that. I found Nico, and I peeled Tom away from Célia's hand to explain the situation. We quickly developed a plan. Phase one: Tom would get Damien's attention by making him think that Célia had told him that Lucie Pichon was in love with him. Are you following me? Phase two: Tom would create a diversion so that Damien would let go of his can. Phase three: Nico would then grab the can and empty it, while I would monitor the entire operation to ensure everything went as expected. Our plan was FOOLPROOF.

We emptied the can and replaced it with soda. Damien didn't notice a thing, but afterward he wouldn't stop clinging to Lucie.

Want to go out with me, Lucie?

Mwah, mwah!

I also took the time to discreetly drop my present off in the middle of the others. After all that effort, I pounced on the food. There were cocktail weenies, mini-pizzas, an entire bowl of Atomics—my favorite candy—and . . . salt and vinegar chips!

Hey, hey, hey! Apparently Naïs knows my weaknesses. That's a good sign! 😜 But the big drag was that her grandma, Mrs. Raymond, was there. 😬 You know, the lady from Reading Passion? When she saw that Nico and I were there, she totally cornered us during the beginning of the evening.

In fact, she really wanted us to sign up for next year—if we didn't, the reading club might not be "renewed" because of the lack of students. Nico and I didn't need to talk it over; doing it again was OUT OF THE QUESTION. 🙁 So when the first song started playing, I sacrificed myself and invited Mrs. Raymond to dance in order to distract her.

Luckily, at one point they put on Master Pim's (a super trendy American rapper), and Raoul started doing this weird dance. He took little steps with his feet and moved his elbows, like he was running a marathon in place.

He told us that he'd seen the dance last summer at a mall in the United States 🗽 and that it was called the "Running Man." According to him, it was about to blow up over here. . . . He made Mathis, Damien, and Lucas do it with him. They looked 🙈 completely ridiculous, 😝 but at least it got me out of dancing with Mrs. Raymond. After about five minutes, Nico was sick of watching them showing off, especially when Lena was all alone on the sidelines. He went to change the music and put on Pink Romance. He took Lena's wheelchair and started turning slowly with her.

As for me, I invited Naïs to dance. 😍 I happen to know Pink Romance is her favorite singer. Hey, hey, hey! THE HIGHLIGHT OF THE NIGHT. It was perfect . . . well, almost, because her grandma wouldn't let us out of her sight. 😬

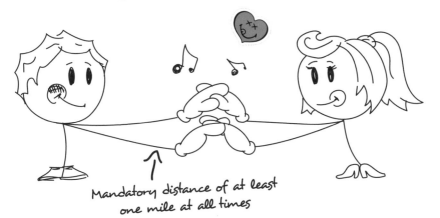

↑ Mandatory distance of at least one mile at all times

But after we danced, I had another issue: I was dying of heat from the lights, the disco ball, and holding hands with Naïs. . . . 😅 So I took off my sweatshirt. But I'd completely forgotten I was wearing my IAG shirt. I thought everyone was going to make fun of me, but actually, believe it or not, everyone at the party thought my T-shirt was super cool! 😁

And so we turned off the music, and Nico made a big announcement. He explained that we were starting a charity and that we were going to organize a sale at the end of the year to collect money for the Welcoming Wheelchairs organization, so that Lena and others with reduced mobility could get a service puppy!

Let's just say it was a big hit. Everyone applauded for us, starting with Lena, Naïs, and Célia. Then I felt Naïs getting closer to me . . . and it's at that exact moment that her grandma came out with the cake. Naïs blew out the candles and unwrapped her presents. But just as she was unwrapping mine, Raoul snatched it from her hands. He laughed and said it reminded him of Mr. Boulfou's hats. Mr. Boulfou is the social studies teacher who made us wear hats when we sang at Pleasant Gardens last year.

Oh no! He opened the zipper to put his head inside the pillow, and he started singing "Hope and Life." But that big doofus pushed too hard, and he couldn't get it off.

So I rushed to the rescue.

HELP!

I pulled off the pillow, and just then I saw my poem was about to

SLIDE DOWN HIS T-SHIRT!

I caught it just in time, and I immediately hid it in the pocket of my jeans. Unfortunately, it was then impossible for me to put it back inside the pillow without being caught. I had to give up! I was so ticked off.

151

At ten o'clock everyone went home. But there was a big problem in the stairwell: the steps were covered with confetti! Another stunt from one of those jerks! When we saw Naïs's grandma's face, Nico and I offered to clean it all up. To tell you the truth, dear future human, I think I scored serious points with Naïs. When we were leaving, she gave me KISS on the cheek and told me I was awesome tonight. Now my only worry is that this morning I looked everywhere in my jeans, and I couldn't find my poem. . . .

Sunday

Dear future human,

Things aren't going very well for one simple reason: I have to kiss IAG goodbye for the time being. You see, I've got another HUGE problem on my hands: Tom and Célia are OVER.

For my part, I'm happy to see that old slug again, but it sucks to see him like this . . . not to mention their relationship had been a serious asset in my crusade for Naïs's love. Long story short, I spent most of the break trying to boost this wimp's morale. How can I put this lightly . . . his heart's been shattered into a thousand pieces.

Everything was going great until Naïs's party, but after that things went south between them. ☹ And it's only because of a box of snails. They got it in their heads to "test their love" by raising some snails together in an old shoebox. Each one had to watch the little guys every other week. But evidently, when Célia got the box back the day after the party, the snails had disappeared without Tom realizing. 😮 And she blew up at him.

😮 Phewwwie! If you want my opinion, girls are complicated. Since Tom was inconsolable, my mom suggested inviting him to Grandpa and Grandma's house in Brittany for a few days. But it was actually a terrible idea, because seeing Marion and Tristan Le Bouzec smooching all day long brought back too many memories for him.

But the worst was when one day we walked by Fastburger and the window still had an ad from the Valentine's Day promotion. 🙁 All of that gave him a nasty case of the blues.

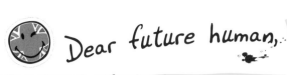 Dear future human, **Saturday**

Our trip to England is coming up: in one month, the whole seventh-grade class will be there! The thought of leaving is good news—I feel like it's about time for a change of scenery.

But all this stalls our IAG plans again. Basically Mr. Cariou, the computer teacher, was supposed to help us start talking with our pen pals again. But guess what—our school's videoconference system <u>doesn't work anymore!</u> No surprise, if you ask me. So the teacher had us brainstorm, in groups of two, "original" ways to communicate with the English middle school that will welcome our class.

We had to write down our ideas on little anonymous slips of paper, then the teacher read them to us. At first there were some good ideas:

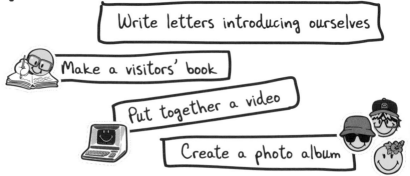

Write letters introducing ourselves

Make a visitors' book

Put together a video

Create a photo album

But then it went down the tubes from there:

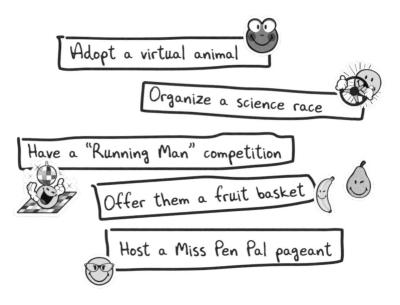

Adopt a virtual animal

Organize a science race

Have a "Running Man" competition

Offer them a fruit basket

Host a Miss Pen Pal pageant

Write down a selection of the best roast beef recipes

Make an acrostic puzzle

Masterful
Amicable
X times full of skills
Intrepid
Meticulous
Euphoric

Rotten
Arrogant
Obnoxious
Unintelligent
Loathsome

Nico and I were lucky enough to have our project chosen. 😉 The idea is to make a big package into which everyone will put a personal object that represents themselves and that will be useful during our exchange. We have one week to prepare it all!

Dear future human,

Coming up with a personal object I could send to that ole Brit Conrad really had me scratching my head 😵 I thought about putting my fur blanket in the package, since it perfectly represents my personality and it'd be useful when I was there. 😁 I could stand to treat myself to this little luxury (especially these days . . .), but when it comes down to it, it's too bulky—and more importantly . . . it smells a bit like basement funk. 😐 So I settled on *Extreme Excavator*, my favorite comic.

It turns out I had a second copy. It was the perfect chance for Conrad to make progress on his French before my arrival. 🙂

Ze extrame excavator rooled at fool sped over everyting een hiss way. It ways a terrayble slooghter.

This past weekend, Tom, Nico, and I <u>urgently</u> met to finalize IAG. At last! Seeing as we're leaving for England soon, we had good reason to hurry. Thankfully, the two wimps seemed to understand this. Nico's mom gave us  instructions for printing the shirts and hats, and we followed them to a T. We should receive our delivery when we get back home. After the England trip, we'll need to organize the charity sale, and I suspect convincing the teachers won't be a cakewalk.

Thursday

We are T-minus ONE DAY from departure, and this morning in computer class we received the package from our pen pals. They had the funny idea to make "riddle portraits" for us. From a bunch of cryptic statements, we had to figure out which English student each sketch described. Needless to say, I didn't have much trouble recognizing Conrad's.

If I were a dish, I'd be ... a cucumber and jelly sandwich.

If I were a video game, I'd be ... Zombieland 2.

If I were a haircut, I'd be ... a mullet.

If I were a soccer player, I'd be ... Pietro.

If I were a French singer, I'd be ... Ben Didji.

If I were a French specialty, I'd be ... stiiinky cheese.

If I were a game, I'd be ... "garbage garb."

If I were a French expression, I'd be ... "I just demolished you, ya ole shriveled slug!"

I'm actually really looking forward to seeing that old redcoat again. We leave tomorrow, and my bags are packed. England, here I come!

APRIL

OPERATION UNION JACK:

COMMENCE
BRIEFING

Dear future human,

Cheerio—I'm back! You can bet your sweet patootie I didn't bring my journal. It was just too risky. Imagine if Raoul came across it?

Anyway, I did try to stuff my furry blanket in my suitcase, but it was physically impossible. I had to stash it under my bed. Anyhow, a ton of stuff happened, but I'll try to focus on the most memorable twists and adventures.

For starters, to get there we all took the bus. Even Lena! Don't ask me how all of that was possible, because going on a school trip with a disabled person is no small feat.

You have to fill out tons of paperwork to get "financial assistance" and "authorizations." A real pain! ☹ What's cool was that Nico volunteered to help Lena whenever she needed and push her wheelchair whenever she was tired. That sounds like something Lisa would have loved to do! ☺

Mr. Crazot, Mr. Cariou, and Ramoupoulos were our chaperones. Raoul and his losers totally stole the back of the bus, and they even had a table so they could have a little picnic! For the entire ride, they wouldn't stop acting like they were at a restaurant and asking Déborah Pouyou and Chloé Dubuc to serve them. We also left an hour late, because Martin Picard didn't hear his alarm clock. This guy is always running late. 😴 It's practically a tradition of his . . . or maybe some kind of rare and unstudied disease. 😬

It's so bad we've started calling him "MIA" Martin! As for pranks, Raoul and his dimwitted gang outdid themselves! Before we left, they rummaged in Paul's bag to pilfer all of his underwear, and they slathered shaving cream on Jules's hands while he was sleeping. When he woke up, he rubbed his eyes and got it all over his face. They also drew in black Sharpie on Nolan's head while he was napping and then took pictures.

Naïs was sitting next to Lena, who Nico and Ramoupoulos had helped get seated. And while Nico was lending a hand, I took the opportunity to toss our backpacks on the seats in front of the girls. Lots of travel time with Naïs behind me! THE ULTIMATE DREAM! 😍 We shared our headphones between the seats, so we could listen to music together. I think I now know every single word to every single Pink Romance song. Who knows how, but Tom and Célia ended up right next to each other. I saw Tom was making some attempts to talk, but the mood was ice-cold.

Conrad's whole class was waiting for us when we finally arrived. From far away, I thought that the old Brit was wearing a construction helmet on his head, but he wasn't actually. Conrad hadn't changed much; he was still the same old Conrad . . . more or less. 😊

Bonjour, Super Sluuug

Mom had made sure I had a little present for Conrad's family—an Eiffel Tower. But when I gave it to his mom, I could see it was going to join their Eiffel Tower collection on the living-room shelf. 😮 Then she gave me a pair of Scottish slippers that were already pretty well worn and a food survey to fill out: the stuff I liked, the stuff I didn't like . . . but for some reason, nothing I liked was ever cooked during my entire stay. But I think in one week, I probably ate food from all of the colors of the rainbow on my sandwiches! 😉

Then Conrad showed me around his house. And it was at that point I had the "privilege" of running into Lydia, his notorious older sister. She was coming out of the bathroom and immediately slammed the door in our faces. Lydia is already annoyyyyying me!

But it's weird, one second later, I thought I heard a guy's voice coming from her room and Lydia laughing. I wondered if Conrad had a brother he'd forgotten to tell me about. Then I decided I was just hallucinating because I was so tired. 😊

We played some *Dogs of Hell*, which I'd managed to stash in my bag. Then I went to take a shower so I could relax for a second. But the shower was really strange. ☹️

It took me a ridiculously long time to figure out how it worked. When the water was finally running, I took my time, lathering up from head to toe. But after ten minutes, there was no more hot water. It was impossible to rinse off. 😮 It was a total disaster, because I was still completely covered in soap. I tried to quietly call out to Conrad, but that old bloke didn't hear me at all. 😬

It was hopeless. And so I had to sneak out of the bathroom holding a hand towel in front of me, but then I ran right into Lydia—who busted out laughing after seeing me totally naked in the hallway.

THE MOST EMBARASSING MOMENT OF MY LIFE!

Then she went back to her room and slammed the door in my face again. But I put my ear to her door and heard this conversation (in English):

> – What is the film *Titanic* about?
> – Which one?
> – *Titanic*.
> – I forget.

With my level of English, maybe I didn't understand everything, but this time I was certain I wasn't dreaming! Plus, the guy she was talking to seemed <u>totally stupid</u>! 😌 I was suddenly worried that I was the only one who suspected an "unknown presence" 👻 in the house. And what if I was right last year about Conrad being shady? <u>And what if his family had been keeping someone prisoner in their house for years?</u> I really started freaking out. 😬

I wanted to warn Conrad . . . At that instant, his mom called us to dinner. I had to give up on rinsing and put on some clothes as fast as I could. And since during dinner they all seemed "<u>normal</u>," I didn't dare say anything. 😐 I probably just needed a good night's sleep to get my head on straight. 😌

The schedule for the week was pretty simple: we had classes at Conrad's middle school in the morning, we went on tours in the afternoon, and we spent a lot of time at the "community center" at night. WITHOUT THE TEACHERS on our backs! 😁 It was a really nice place, a little like the YMCA where Nico goes. There were some badminton courts, and it turns out I'm pretty good at that game! But most importantly, there was a cafeteria. It was the spot to meet up with Nico, Naïs, Lena, Tom, Célia, and their hosts: Diana, Amy, Gary, etc. By the way, they'd all been super lucky, because they were all neighbors! Conrad, on the other hand, lives miles away in the middle of nowhere. 🙁

One night, we came back later than we thought because Tom's pen pal, Wilson, had organized a little party at his house. Conrad's parents were already asleep, because they have to get up super early for work.

Lydia was supposed to make sure we came home safe and sound, but when we got back, the deadbolt was locked and Lydia had even put the keys inside! Conrad knocked and knocked and sent a text to his parents, but everyone was asleep. Basically, <u>WE WERE GOING TO SPEND THE NIGHT OUTSIDE!</u> And, of course, it was raining and freezing cold. Then Conrad suddenly had a brilliant idea as he looked at the flower garden bushes still draped in their protective covers from the winter.

I was sorry I couldn't read *Children Soft as Pandas*, because this whole ordeal had totally stressed me out. But I actually fell asleep right away. The next day, I got an email from my parents on Conrad's family computer. It cheered me up. In fact, I was starting to miss them. But when I looked closer, I saw there was an attachment. When I opened it, I was so

ANNOYYYYYYED!!!...

Anyway, I'm not going to go on about my sister, especially when I saw that Conrad isn't really much better off.

Guess what—I'd almost forgotten about the voice in Lydia's room, when the second-to-last night at Conrad's house I heard a deep voice:

- Do you have a girlfriend?
- You could say I have something going on, even a few somethings.
- I love you.
- That's nice. Can we get back to work now?
- Will you marry me?
- I already have everything I need.
- You're getting on my nerves!
- Take a deep breath.
- Leave me alone!
- It would be more polite to say, "goodbye."

OK, I know my English grade is just barely pushing a C, but I was certain I'd understood the conversation (and I'm rather proud of my translation here). And I can assure you none of it made any sense. Then all of a sudden, I thought: "Jackpot! Lydia is hiding a boyfriend in her room!" But what I couldn't quite figure out was why we'd never seen him!

This time I ran off to find Conrad and tell him what was going on . . . or at least try to. I imitated the exchange, and we went to listen to the rest of the conversation.

- Do the Chicken Dance!
- I don't dance. These darn feet don't have any sense of rhythm. Besides, I don't have any feet!
- Can I call you darling?
- OK, but everyone else calls me Riri.

Conrad started laughing hysterically and pulled me into his room. Then he started making these wild gestures. Only I didn't understand anything he was trying to say. So he took out his cell phone and started talking to it. And guess what—the telephone started answering him!

- Does Santa exist?
- Really, Conrad, I'm surprised you would ask!

Eventually, Conrad explained that Riri was the name of a speech recognition app. . . . So in a nutshell, Lydia was talking to her phone and giving it orders with her voice! You can bet that I, with my old Niphon, didn't know something like that could possibly exist. 😃

OK, dear future human, I know, I know. You must be making fun of me now that you've just read this humiliating incident! I hope you'll never talk about it with anyone else. Pinky swear? 😉

Anyway, we spent our last day in London. It took almost two hours to drive there, and we nearly missed the changing of the guards. But except for tufts of black fur that stuck out above the crowd, we didn't see much. For lunch, we had an orange mush sandwich. It was really weird. 😕

Conrad kept trying to explain it to me in French, showing me the inside of the sandwich. "Malade! Malade!" he said, which means "Sick! Sick!" I wasn't 100% sure what he meant, but to be on the safe side I decided to toss my sandwich. Before I did though, Tom clarified that it was actually "MARMALADE," a specialty there.

Anyhow, it had an orange flavor, and, to tell you the truth, it was . . . really not bad. Then we visited Madame Tussauds wax museum, and the good news is that there was a statue of Pietro. Look! Conrad took a photo of me.

At the end of the day, we had some free time on Oxford Street. Dad and Mom had exchanged some money for me, but you can probably guess I ran into serious trouble in the stores. 😕 Someone should've told me beforehand that British money makes no sense: the big coins are the cents—practically worthless—and the little coins are worth a few bucks! 😃 Thankfully, Tom was with me, and he explained it all before I looked like a thief and permanently ruined the reputation of the French abroad. In short, all of that is to tell you that I used my free time to get some souvenirs:

peppermint sauce for Marion

little teddy bear for Lisa

marmalade for me!

tea for Mom

umbrella for Dad

When we met up in front of the bus, Mr. Crazot started counting us. Disaster! Four students were missing: Raoul, Damien, Mathis, and . . . "MIA" Martin. I was afraid most of all for him. The teachers asked us where they were last seen. That's when Lena and Nico said they remembered spotting the guys at Piccadilly Circus.

One hour later, we saw Mr. Ramoupoulos return with Raoul, his morons, and Martin—soaked from head to toe. We found out afterward that Raoul didn't have any money left for our free time. That big idiot had spent it all in the cafeteria at the community center, offering soda to Alison (his pen pal) to impress her. So he'd forced Martin to collect all the coins in the fountain!

Believe me, they were seriously punished. In the bus on our way back to France, Ramoupoulos, Cariou, and Crazot made all four of them sit in the front to keep an eye on them. 😀 At the time I didn't think it was really fair to Martin. After all, he was only a victim in the whole thing. 🙂 But I realized later that there was another reason for that after all. . . .

BARF
BAG

RAOUL IS
THE BEST

The good news is that all six of us—Lena, Naïs, Tom, Célia, Nico, and I—could sit in the back of the bus. 😍 We listened to music.

Lena told us a bunch of stories about her misadventures, like the time her wheelchair got stuck right in the middle of a crosswalk—which caused a mega traffic jam. Then there's public transportation or the nasty remarks she hears sometimes, like when the restaurant staff didn't give her a menu because they weren't sure she could read, or the time a friend asked her in front of the whole class how she goes to the bathroom, or the strangers who tell her, "Keep it up!" and "Good Luck!" 🙁 I'd never thought about all these struggles, and I realized Tom's words on the wall were right: stupidity is everywhere. 😈

Eventually, she imitated Raoul doing the Running Man, and that made us all laugh.

Nico, Tom, and I told them all about IAG, and we said our first mission when we got back was to convince the teachers to let us hold a sale to benefit the Welcoming Wheelchairs charity.

I noticed the vibe between Tom and Célia was more relaxed than on the way there, and after a while, Naïs fell asleep. Dear future human, I think it was the best day of my life.

OPERATION UNION JACK:

TERMINATE BRIEFING

Wednesday   Dear future human,

Tom and I spent the afternoon at Nico's house. He got the T-shirts and hats! Complete success! This is gonna be <u>epic</u>!

Now all that's left is to find a way to persuade the teachers to organize the fundraiser during the end-of-the-year school party. And believe me, unless there's a miracle, I have no idea how we're going to convince them!

HUGE NEWS!

Today was our last day of Reading Passion, and Mrs. Raymond, Naïs's grandma, saved a special surprise for us. 😁 Guess what? The winner of the readers' choice contest was *Cannibal Burger*. But something even better happened when we arrived: the author, Gad Slimaud, was right there, sitting behind a desk! A literary star! Can you believe it? SWEET! 😁 I have to admit it bumped my motivation up a notch. We took the chance to ask him a ton of questions:

✓ How did he know he wanted to write books?

✓ Where does he find inspiration?

✓ Do you have to have disheveled hair and wear glasses to be a writer?

✓ What's it like to be famous?

✓ How did he get the idea for his first book, *War of the Noodles*?

✓ Does he believe in aliens?

It was honestly really interesting. At the end he offered us each a signed copy of *Cannibal Burger*. So cool!

Right as we were about to leave, Mrs. Raymond asked Nico and me to stay. I was terrified she'd make us sign up for the club again next year. Then Gad Slimaud came out from behind the desk, and we then had the surprise of a lifetime!

Don't ask me the <u>details</u> of <u>why</u> or <u>how</u> this <u>crazy coincidence</u> could happen, but basically Mrs. Raymond arranged everything. 😛 It turns out that, after her party, Naïs told her grandma all about our IAG project. So Mrs. Raymond immediately thought to invite Gad Slimaud, who, in addition to being a writer, is also the president of a little thing called Welcoming Wheelchairs. Can you believe it? 😃

And the best part: not only was the charity ready to help us but also Mrs. Raymond got permission from the principal of the middle school for us to have our sale at the end-of-the-year party!

I'm telling you, it's crazy!

Dear future human,

After everything I told you about last time, I've been really busy between the end of school, tests, and especially 😖 preparation for the charity sale. Nico, Tom, and I have been more overwhelmed than ever! Especially since Tom still hasn't gotten over his "separation" from Célia, so he's been doing everything <u>extremely slowly</u>, like the big slug he is. 😠 Thankfully, with my parents' permission, we turned the garage into IAG headquarters. You should've seen the mess we had in there . . . between the boxes of T-shirts and hats, the banners, and the stand we made. It had taken over all our weekends, but it was even better than in *Middle School Madness*. Naïs and Lena even came by at one point to see us. 😊

The big day is tomorrow, and I have some serious butterflies!

It's crazy how in only forty-eight hours, 😬 so much can happen to one person. I have TONS of stuff to tell you. Yesterday was the most incredible day of my entire existence. Tom, Nico, and I showed up to school super early and set up our IAG stand. The place was deserted. It didn't start out so great, because the only spot the principal had reserved for us wasn't exactly in the middle of the playground.

Let's just say the odor that was wafting out from the bathroom was absolutely terrifying. 😬 At least once we hung everything up, our stand looked great. ⭐⭐⭐⭐⭐⭐

Then we lucked out, because Raoul turned up, clearly having just applied some cheap cologne. And believe me, he'd really outdone himself. I don't know how, but Nico managed to sucker him into being one of our models and wearing some of our clothes. This vain bozo didn't need to be asked twice—he was convinced all the girls from school would fall for him. But what he didn't know was that we'd ONLY asked him to be our model to mask the smell coming from the bathroom with his "fragrance." 🌼

Little by little, the school filled up. 😃 Thanks to the help from the teachers and all the other students, we were able to recruit lots of people for our fundraiser. Practically the whole school wanted to help Welcoming Wheelchairs and help disabled people adopt service dogs. But we wanted most of all to show Lena that <u>we're all supporting her!</u> 😊

Naïs, Lena, and Célia were also running a cake stand. At one point, they brought a piece of cake for each of us . . . even Raoul, which wasn't really necessary if you ask me. 🙁

And, coincidence or not, Naïs made licorice gingerbread. . . . Think back—does that remind you of anything that might have happened around this time last year? 😉 I'm sure she winked at me right when she gave me a piece.

"MIA" Martin was supposed to have a toy sale, but he didn't show up till noon. 😜 Mrs. Raymond and Mrs. Toinou hosted a reading workshop promoting *Cannibal Burger*.

Not to brag, but our stand was by far the most popular. 😁 To give you an idea, I guess you could say . . . it was the RAID OF THE CENTURY! We sold everything!

In the schoolyard, <u>almost everyone was wearing a smiley hat or T-shirt that read,</u> <u>"It's All Good!"</u> Not that I'm easily moved by this kind of thing, but honestly, "The impression was striking," as Gad Slimaud might say.

Speaking of which, around three o'clock an enormous truck pulled up in front of the school. The principal opened the door, and Gad got out with two hefty guys. Inside the truck were five wheelchairs.

Oh yes! 😃 I forgot to tell you, all that was Nico's brilliant idea. After the last meeting of Reading Passion, he asked Gad if it would be possible for Welcoming Wheelchairs to lend us a few wheelchairs for a "roll race." 😊 The best way to raise awareness among "normal" people is to put them in the shoes of "disabled" 🤔 people, don't you think?

Gad Slimaud gave the green light right away! And that's how we found ourselves taking part in a wheelchair race with Lena as the star instructor. She, Nico, and even Ramoupoulos had organized an obstacle course with gym equipment. But of course, Raoul wanted to be the <u>first</u> to try it. 😠 He sat down, and I thought for sure he was about to play bumper cars with his three goons, but the idiot couldn't even move forward.

Raoul: he talks all tough, but when it comes to muscles, he's all show! He was getting so worked up that he fell forward . . . and started crying like a big baby. That was the best! It was Lena who helped him get up. Then <u>something happened that I never thought possible:</u>

Then, Inès and Fatiha tried to connect their chairs together, but they never got past the starting line. For the last race, Nico, Tom, Célia, Naïs, and I all readied our chairs.

Nico asked Lena to join in the race too, and obviously she crossed the finish line first while the rest of us were stuck in front of the fences that framed the trees in the courtyard. Afterward, I found my parents and Lisa. I introduced my little sister to Lena, because I knew she dreamed of trying out a wheelchair someday. It was now or never. 😄 Fifteen minutes later I saw them doing the obstacle course together, then Lisa pushed Lena like she was her doll. Needless to say, they looked like they were having a lot of fun. 😁

Then the principal made a seemingly endless speech about disability, the "necessity" of events like today, and . . . the pride 😁 he felt to have "significantly contributed." Finally, he brought out a big box and told everyone that we'd managed to collect a <u>small fortune</u> for Welcoming Wheelchairs.

Gad Slimaud thanked us on behalf of the organization and said that, because of us, many more people would soon be able to adopt a service dog to help them with their daily lives. Everyone applauded loudly  for us. An hour later, it was time to clean up. On our stand there were over a dozen empty boxes, and I saw Tom disappear with one of them. I thought he had a lot of nerve to ditch us again right when we needed his help the most. But fifteen minutes later, he returned with the box still under his arms.

And instead of putting it in the trash, he gave it to Célia.

Eternal love

TOM + Célia

↑ Snail box made by Super Slug!

At the end of the day, Célia left with Tom. Nico walked Lena home. And I found myself alone with Naïs. I don't know how, but I mustered the courage to ask her to leave with me. 🙂 I was afraid she'd turn me down, but she actually gave me a big smile.

😀

On the way home, I was trying to find all sorts of intelligent things to say to her, but the more I thought about it, the less came to me. When we were close to her house, she told me she was really impressed with our generosity toward Lena and Welcoming Wheelchairs. I wanted to say, "You know, Naïs, I have something to tell you . . . I've been in love with you since last year," but for some reason my throat was completely frozen. Then, suddenly, she confessed that after her party, she found a piece of paper on the ground in the elevator . . . MY POEM! 😮

And before I could think of anything to say, one last thing happened that I wasn't expecting AT ALL. <u>Naïs kissed me!</u> Yes, yes! I swear! It was too amazing to be real!

My fear of being an astronaut lost in space became a sweet dream. I saw myself floating on a cloud, surrounded by shooting stars. And believe me, it was one thousand times better than being bundled up in my furry blanket. I tried to covertly pinch myself to make sure it was actually real, but I missed and accidentally pinched Naïs's arm! What was also scary was that I kept my eyes open at first, before I remembered that in movies lovers always close their eyes when they kiss. I hope I wasn't making a stupid face.

Anyway, two seconds later, Mrs. Raymond showed up, and we had to tell her how the day turned out. And that's how I found out Naïs was going back to Brittany this summer. Before we parted ways, she said something that really made me happy:

So I don't think I'm wrong to say I'm officially GOING OUT with Naïs!

The End

Dear future human,

There you have it, seventh grade is already in the past! And even if the year started out bad, I think it was all good in the end . . . ONCE AGAIN!!! 🙂 Raoul Kador stayed true to himself (unfortunately), and Conrad? Well . . . he's still Conrad. My friendship with Tom almost went to pieces, but meeting Nico was a game changer. This guy is really great! 😮 I supported a cause that was totally worth it . . . and I'm more than a little proud of that! And above all, my wish came true—I kissed a girl for the first time in my entire life, and it wasn't just anyone! 😉 Conclusion: I'm dedicating this year to you, Mom. I never thanked you enough for signing me up for Reading Passion. All this is actually thanks to you.

Oh! One more piece of good news: this morning in front of the mirror, I spotted something very interesting.

I can now tell you that, without a doubt, putting deodorant on your cheeks does NOT make you grow a beard! It's true . . . nature knows best! 😉 Tom, Nico, and I went to the vacant lot. We had a hard time finding the place where Tom and I had hidden our box of memories from last year.

But we were eventually able to get our hands on it, and it really made us laugh to see the police sketch of Conrad, the advertisement for *Zombieland 2*, 😊 and all of the other memories from sixth grade. Then we started over. Our seventh-grade "time capsule" was ready to be buried.

We had a moment of silence in front of our box, and then we piled the dirt on top of it.

Now the real question: what does next year have in store for me, dear future human? 🤔 But . . . who cares in the end, since I got this . . . mostly! 😉

Andrews McMeel Publishing
a division of Andrews McMeel Universal
1130 Walnut Street, Kansas City, Missouri 64106

www.andrewsmcmeel.com

18 19 20 21 22 SDB 10 9 8 7 6 5 4 3 2 1
ISBN: 978-1-4494-9571-8
Library of Congress Control Number: 2018940511

Made by:
Shenzhen Donnelley Printing Company Ltd.
Address and location of manufacture:
No. 47, Wuhe Nan Road, Bantian Ind. Zone,
Shenzhen, China, 518129
1st Printing—7/23/18

Editor: Jean Z. Lucas
Art Director/Designer: Diane Marsh
Production Manager: Chuck Harper
Production Editor: Kevin Kotur
Translators: Leigh-Ann Haggerty and Kevin Kotur

ATTENTION: SCHOOLS AND BUSINESSES
Andrews McMeel books are available at quantity discounts with
bulk purchase for educational, business, or sales promotional use.
For information, please e-mail the Andrews McMeel Publishing
Special Sales Department: specialsales@amuniversal.com.